The Other Dashwood Sister

A Jane Austen Sequel

Miranda Markwell

Bryant Street Publishing

Chapter One

Miss Margaret Dashwood was used to being last. The youngest of the three Dashwood sisters, Margaret's adolescent and adult life had been punctuated by *waiting*: waiting for the formal mourning period to end after her father died, waiting for her sisters to marry, waiting for her mother to recover once Marianne and Elinor left with their new husbands, waiting for her sisters to have children, and waiting for invitations to visit those children once they were born. For many years, Margaret had waited for the opportunity to come out in London as a young, marriageable woman, but the whole ordeal had been rather disappointing.

In all her waiting, though, Margaret had resolved at a young age that there was one thing she would *never* deign to wait for: a gentleman.

This decision had been formed while watching her older sisters court their own future husbands, an episode of her life that she wished never to repeat. What she had noticed the most about Marianne and Elinor's experience of courtship was that they had had almost no control over any of its ups and downs. They were passive participants in a dance that left them dependent upon whether a strong dance partner would show up and lead. To their credit, Mr. Ferrars and Colonel Brandon *had* finally made their intentions known and whisked her sisters away to wifehood, but the interim time had left the Dashwood sisters powerless in their dejected melancholy.

Margaret was never melancholy. On the contrary, she was stubbornly glad most of the time, intent upon letting good things happen to her at every opportunity. This was perhaps her greatest attribute. Or her tragic flaw.

Her firm resistance against melancholy was a learned behavior, one that she cultivated in order to protect herself from the danger she had witnessed in her own sisters' depression. When Marianne found herself disappointed by a man who pledged his love but not his hand, she fell into a deep well of melancholic fatigue that nearly killed her. Margaret had not been by Marianne's bedside when the worst of the illness occurred, and she had always felt frustration at having been a young girl who was tucked away at home rather than on the front lines of her sister's convalescence. But she understood the seriousness of this past illness, one that neither Elinor, Marianne, nor their mother ever wished to speak of. This episode had taught her that lovesickness could kill, and she resolved never to let herself fall into this method of reaching death's door.

Margaret's constitution, however, was fundamentally different from that of her two sisters — especially from the overwhelmingly emotional Marianne. Margaret was always in motion, rarely lonely, and much more content with a visit to a London zoo than the anticipation of a family dinner with a handsome, wealthy gentleman. The baby of the family, she had grown up receiving an excess of attention, and thus she moved through the world with an expectation of being seen. During her season of coming out in London, however, she had been frustrated with the vapidity of the whole affair, a season of being on display that made her feel more like chattel than a young woman in want of a helpmeet. Margaret rarely cared for her looks, but her season in London made her newly aware of her freckles and sunny orange hair, physical traits to which she had previously given little thought.

In London at eighteen years old, Margaret learned something her family had known all along: she was anything but *demure*, a characteristic that seemed to be in high demand among the young men seeking wives. Margaret's physical appearance heightened the revelation of her exuberance, which only made the more timid men retreat in something that approached intimidation. The gentlemen who possessed a bit more boldness found her to be an excellent addition to any lively conversation, but this attention appeared to stop short of categorizing her as an object of flirtation.

So Margaret found herself in a conundrum: there did not seem to be any middle ground between being terrifying and being one of the chaps.

This response surprised Margaret tremendously — and with good reason, too. In the several years before her eighteenth birthday, Margaret had enjoyed the company of two very wise and thoughtful gentlemen: her sisters' husbands. Edward Ferrars (married to Elinor) and Colonel Brandon (married to Marianne) had shown Margaret a brotherly love that instilled in her confidence and poise. They treated her as an intelligent human being, indulged her determination to always enjoy herself, and challenged her when her excitement interfered with her critical thinking. In short, they gave Margaret rather high expectations for what a desirable gentleman might be like. And *none* of the men she encountered during her coming out in London seemed to measure up.

Margaret wondered if her standards were too high, but her understanding of the importance of marriage made her confident that she needed to be picky. It was not so much that she didn't find the men she met in London attractive. Rather, it was a sense that none of them truly viewed her as an intellectual equal. Margaret, a voracious reader, had grown up in houses filled with libraries and had spent the days of her adolescence consumed with a giant atlas of the world. When she was younger, in fact, she had been convinced that she would grow up to be a pirate. When courting her sister, Edward had indulged Margaret's wish and made sure to fill her mind with visions of faraway lands and seas. While in London, though, Margaret realized that the most traveling these soon-to-be-wed young women would do was the standard European Tour that would follow their wedding day. It was considered a grand tour throughout Europe, but not necessarily throughout the rest of the world. Margaret, for her part, was curious about Africa, the Americas, and even the faraway islands where her brother-in-law, Colonel Brandon, had once traveled.

The standard trip to Rome and Paris intrigued her, but it did not excite her in the same way that an African safari roused her spirits. Margaret longed for adventure, but it was becoming ever clearer to her that her life in the English countryside had very little excitement to offer — other than new neighbors, teatime gossip, and long walks on the moors. Although her sisters (especially Marianne) had married comfortably, Margaret and her mother were not wealthy. They were comfortable, but they still had to be mindful of their expenses and to take care that they had enough resources to ensure their comfort for a long while. Mrs. Dashwood had raised some suggestions to Margaret about making a wealthy match, but when Margaret protested that her sisters had not been required to do the same, Mrs. Dashwood relented.

"Mother, I wish you would leave me alone on

the subject of marriage," said Margaret.

"I'm only trying to encourage you to take up some sort of situation of comfort," replied Mrs. Dashwood, who was always concerned about the security of her daughters. After having the two eldest safely ensconced in their comfortable marriages, Mrs. Dashwood was now turning her attention to the young Margaret. The trouble was that Margaret was not so young anymore. Even though she had endured a season in London at age eighteen, Margaret had in fact spent the past ten years single — so single, in truth, that few gentlemen had even gotten within ten feet of Margaret since her time in London.

Mrs. Dashwood was at a loss for why Margaret seemed so resistant to the pleasures of matrimony, especially since her sisters modeled such a strong example of what a happy marriage could be like. But Margaret was resolute. She was not ready to be married, and she made that clear to her mother. Mrs. Dashwood knew well enough not to put pressure on her children when it came to money. The four of them had endured enough financial scarcity when Mrs. Dashwood's late husband had passed away. Her stepson had provided for them in a reasonable manner, but it wasn't exactly generous. Elinor and Marianne, then, had entered adulthood with a sense that marriage was the one way for them to find a sense of security. Margaret, on the other hand, had the benefit of knowing that, if she ever wanted for anything, she could simply appeal to her older sisters and their husbands. And she felt no guilt about this either; Margaret was quite easy to take care of. She was not vain, she did not obsess over possessions (other than books and maps), and she wasn't interested in fine things like dresses and jewelry. Margaret was almost puritan in her way of being in the world, but she would have preferred the language of "efficient."

"My dear, when I was married, I found matrimony to be one of the most exciting adventures of my life," said Mrs. Dashwood. "The care of you and your sisters was a beautiful period of my life. I'm a little sad to be done with it. And your late father was a good man. I cannot stress enough how valuable it is to build a partnership with someone you respect. You're a smart woman, Margaret, and I would think that you would see sense in a marriage of true minds."

"Please don't quote Shakespeare to me, Mother, especially when it's taken completely out of context."

Her mother had been referring, of course, to Shakespeare's famous Sonnet 116, which reads "let me not to the marriage of true minds admit impediments." It's a beautiful poem, a poem often read at weddings and sometimes tucked away deep in love letters. But Margaret knew the poem well enough to know that it wasn't necessarily a poem about what love *was*. It was a poem about what love was *not*. The poem was filled with words like *no, not, neither,* and *never*: "Let me *not* to the marriage of true minds admit impediments." It left a space open for what true love might actually be like. Margaret found this interesting, but she did not find the line "a marriage of true minds" to be a convincing enough reason for joining herself financially and legally to another human being.

"My dear," continued Mrs. Dashwood, "at this point I will quote whomever I need to quote in order to get you to pay attention."

"Mother, you mustn't worry. We are secure here at the cottage, and we're comfortable, don't you think?"

"As you age, Margaret, I have a sense that you may come to see that there are things of much greater importance than the bare minimum of comfort. Some people *do* enjoy luxury, you know."

"I enjoy luxury, mother," replied Margaret. "I know the luxury of books and of writing and of using my imagination. That's serviceable enough luxury for me."

Mrs. Dashwood, who was not a great reader, replied, "I wonder how much you will think it is a luxury when you suddenly need spectacles in order to make out the words on the pages of your books."

I quite like the look of spectacles, thought Margaret, who believed that more women should wear them to begin with. This observation was consistent with Margaret's personality. Once she had discovered, as a very young woman, that her physical appearance was different from the other women around her, she found herself interested in making it even more different. Ten years' time had given her the kind of confidence that comes from being on one's own. For an entire decade, she had dressed herself only to impress herself. She had no interest in impressing others — or *pleasing* them, for that matter. Margaret would have loved a pair of spectacles, but in fact her eyesight was perfect and so she did not need them. In order to embellish herself, then, she often took the time to find just the right flower to tuck into her bun or the perfect black ribbon to wrap around her wrist in a kind of coiled bracelet. None of this was particularly fashionable, but it was different. And Margaret liked being different. She had heard stories of fashionable women who were able to paint their nails with a special kind of lacquer designed for such a thing. Margaret, unfortunately, had never been able to get her hands on this particular product, even in London, but she longed for the day she would find her own tiny bottle of green paint to adorn her nails.

Her mother probably would have died of shock if Margaret had shown up with green fingernails, so Margaret kept that desire to herself. Margaret had other habits, too, that were odd enough to discomfit her mother. She enjoyed wearing men's boots, especially boots that seemed like they had a touch of military flair. She also enjoyed wearing black — it made the flowers and ribbons that she loved stand out so much more. It also made her look like she was in mourning for her existence, but that wasn't entirely true. Margaret liked the seriousness of black, and she liked how the black contrasted against her freckled face and her orange hair. Margaret's older sisters, Elinor and Marianne, had been considered true beauties. It was not so much that Margaret was not beautiful; it was just that she had no desire to conform to the beauty standards that her sisters had fallen into quite naturally.

Margaret had some hopes that the way she dressed made it so that any gentleman who came into contact with her never had the chance to consider her as a "marriageable young woman." Margaret wanted to be taken seriously, and now that she was 28 years old and an old maid in her mother's eyes, she felt this desire with a renewed sense of strength. To her great dismay, the past ten years had taught her that young women (especially if they have some degree of good looks) would not be taken seriously, but instead would be assumed to be either "quiet" or "silly." Margaret was neither. Although she did not consider herself silly, she still had a sense of humor. Margaret loved to laugh, and she especially loved to laugh at great wit. She had no interest in laughing at other people's trouble or at unfortunate gossip. This laughter, to her, seemed to be of a lesser degree. No, Margaret Dashwood enjoyed laughing at things that *surprised* her in some ways. This was Margaret's chief desire in life: *to be surprised.* Her life in the cottage with her mother was very simple, and so the opportunity for a surprise rarely seemed to come around.

When she was eighteen years old and first coming out in London, there had been a small part of herself that wanted to be surprised by another human. And the scene for "surprise" was quite ideal: That first ball in London made her feel starry-eyed. The best part of the evening was not the conversation but the wine and the dancing. Margaret loved activity, and dancing certainly satisfied this desire. She remembered the candlelight and the air smelling like vanilla and cloves. She remembered feeling fresh and sparkling in an emerald gown, and she was pleased with her decision to ornament her hair with tiny sprigs of holly. If there was ever an opportunity for a young woman to fall in love, then this was certainly the scene in which it would happen.

Was it possible that a young man could surprise Margaret Dashwood with a pang of affection? As it turned out, the answer to that question was no. None of the young men surprised her. Many of them, for their part, could not keep up with Margaret Dashwood. Margaret understood the social ritual of coming out in London. She knew full well that every single dance invitation she accepted from a young man was also a kind of consideration of the possibility of marriage. That was the way the world worked. So, instead of ignoring the fact,

Margaret decided that she would simply acknowledge it. This meant that some of her dance part-
ners became overwhelmed when Margaret asked
questions about what they thought of how the
law determined property rights between married
men and women. When Margaret was old enough
to learn of such things, she had been horrified to
discover that, once she was married to a man, she
would essentially become that man's property —
if not in spirit, then at least in the eyes of the law.
This thought was ridiculous to Margaret. If *this*
was how the law viewed marriage, then women to
some degree had a legal status similar to slaves,
and Margaret detested slavery. No one else ever
wished to speak of it, mind you, because it did not
align with the conventions of propriety. But Margaret was happy to bring up the cause whenever
she was provoked. This meant that some of her
dances with the young men in London included
long discussions (guided by Margaret) about the
value of the abolition movement, something that
was still somewhat in its early stages. To be interested in abolition was not fashionable in Margaret's social circles, but Margaret did not care.

Hardly any of the young gentlemen that she
danced with or had a long conversation with in
London seemed to rise to the occasion of Margaret's inquiries. Instead, they were all rather
dull. The conversations that Margaret had with
her mother over breakfast were a thousand times
more interesting than the "conversations" she had

while dancing in London.

Margaret did have a few treasured memories from her season in London, and those memories returned to her over the next decade of her life while she tried to stake out space for herself in the world of potential spinsterhood. She could remember her first ball of that long-ago season, one held at the home of a family friend who had an expansive great hall perfect for these sorts of London affairs. Margaret had been so excited to legitimately be the center of attention. That was often what she wanted the most, especially at eighteen. She felt confident that she was interesting, different, and even a little beautiful. She likewise felt that she had an advantage over her older sisters because she understood what to avoid in a young man.

But her favorite memory of that night had nothing to do with love. It had everything to do with Rupert. Rupert Smith had found his way to this ball by way of his good friend Charles. Charles was a gentleman with a well-established estate. He was also quite young and was on the hunt for a wife. Rupert was from more modest means and had no real interest in marriage. He had just finished his studies at university, a literary scholar who intended to go on to be a professor. He was a specialist in Shakespeare, who was one of Margaret's favorite authors. While trying to find a corner to cool down in toward the end of the ball, Margaret had wandered into the library of the home and found Rupert engrossed in an old and dusty concordance of Shakespeare.

At eighteen years old, Margaret looked her age. She looked like a young woman at the tail end of adolescence and the very beginning of womanhood. Rupert, for his part, still looked like a child. He was small, boyish, and likely never had to worry about facial hair. Rupert, though a bit older than Margaret, looked more like he was fourteen, and yet he had just finished university. At that point in his life, Rupert had very little interest in courting women. He was much more interested in courting great ideas about literature. When Margaret found him, she actually surprised him by quietly walking up behind him and reading the entries in the concordance over his shoulder. An unannounced sneeze made Rupert catapult himself five feet into the air, surprised to find a glowing young woman standing behind him. After the initial shock of their meeting, Margaret and Rupert settled into a conversation that might be compared to a "marriage of true minds" but was not at all romantic.

Margaret and Rupert very likely did not know *how* to be romantic. But they did know how to talk, and talk they did for the remainder of the ball. They shared ideas about literature, quoted from Shakespeare, and argued about different interpretations of the most obscure characters that only the two of them seemed to care about. When Margaret left the ball that first night in London, she did not feel that she had met a gentleman; she felt that she had made a friend. And friends they remained.

For the next ten years, Margaret and Rupert had kept up their correspondence, as well as a few coveted in-person visits with one another. This year, though, was particularly special because Rupert was on a yearlong sabbatical from the university. He had chosen his sabbatical location as a small cottage in the vicinity of the cottage that belonged to Margaret and her mother. His intention was to spend the year compiling all of the notes that he had accumulated over several years of teaching and researching into a book about Shakespeare's history plays. Rupert loved the histories. Margaret preferred comedy and tragicomedy, and she often reminded Rupert that the histories had a profound lack of female characters. Regardless of his questionable taste, though, Margaret was happy to have her friend nearby. She had looked forward to this year for a long time. She had known that a sabbatical was coming for Rupert, and when the letter finally arrived stating his intentions, she nearly overturned the breakfast table in all of her excitement.

Mrs. Dashwood was convinced that Margaret and Rupert would eventually marry. After all, it was unusual for a young man and a young woman (even if both of them were on the wrong side of twenty-five) to be writing letters to one another. Indeed, this was often seen as a sign that the couple was engaged. But Margaret and Rupert were not a romantic couple — they were *friends*. Margaret had to remind her mother of this on an almost daily basis, or at least whenever she received a letter from Rupert

"And what has Rupert written today?" asked Mrs. Dashwood. It was only a few mornings before Rupert was set to arrive in their village for his sabbatical.

"Nothing of great consequence," said Margaret. "Only that he is trying to decide just how many books he needs for a year's time. I told him five trunks would probably be adequate, but he is unsure."

"Five trunks of books!" exclaimed Mrs. Dashwood. "It's almost as if he's moving in, not staying for the span of time it takes to write a book."

"Mother, it is a yearlong sabbatical," said Margaret. "He needs all of the resources he can get his hands on, especially if he is going to write the book well."

"And will he have time to visit with you if his chief goal is to, as you say, write the book well?"

"Oh, Mother, don't you see that I will be helping him write the book?"

"Helping him?" said Mrs. Dashwood.

"Yes, of course!" continued Margaret. "Part of the reason he's coming to our village is so that he can have my editorial and readerly support."

"You intend to *help* him?" asked a surprised Mrs. Dashwood. "I thought you only meant to *visit* with him."

"Is that all you think I am good for, mother? Visiting with acquaintances?"

"Oh no, my darling, you're good at very many things, but I do find you to be an excellent visiting companion when we make our calls."

"Mother," said Margaret, "while Rupert is here this year, I will probably not be as available for all of our visiting calls. I will be helping him write."

Mrs. Dashwood paused over her tea, using a tiny spoon to swirl the milk around. "Margaret...," she began.

"Yes, Mother?"

"You really mean to tell me that you are not in love with Mr. Rupert Smith?"

"No, Mother, I am not in love with Mr. Rupert Smith. We are friends — dear friends — and I am going to help him write a *magnificent* book."

And then Mrs. Dashwood said a surprising thing. "But, my dear, are you really helping him write the book? Won't his name be on the title at the end of it?"

Margaret smiled. "That may be his plan now, but I have a feeling that he will find my insights so valuable and my editorial intervention so pointed that he may have no choice but to designate me as a coauthor."

"And does Rupert know of your designs?" asked Mrs. Dashwood.

Margaret laughed. "He will know of them eventually, and I have no doubt that he will be pleased."

Mrs. Dashwood loved her daughter's confidence, but she sometimes wished that she would be a little *less* confident, especially when it came to the egos of gentlemen. Mrs. Dashwood liked Rupert. She had met Rupert several times and found him to be an interesting, respectable, and kind young man. They had long ago ceased upholding the formality of calling him "Mr. Smith" in their conversations concerning him — he had become a true intimate of the Dashwoods, if only from a distance. She felt that he respected her youngest child. But his attentions to her daughter made her wonder immensely whether or not he was desperately in love with Margaret. In ten years' time, however, he had never so much as hinted at a romantic attraction to Margaret. Mrs. Dashwood did not know whether to be frustrated or grateful that Rupert Smith had never proposed to Margaret. She wondered if it had something to do with Rupert's finances. He was not a member of the landed gentry, but he was not a church mouse either. Her other fear was that Rupert felt insecure about *Margaret's* finances, which could have been the reason he never broached the topic of marriage. Mrs. Dashwood really was at a loss for why Rupert did not seem interested in marrying Margaret. It made more sense to her why Margaret had no interest in marrying Rupert. After all, Margaret acted as if she had no interest in marrying *anyone*, and it annoyed Mrs. Dashwood to no end.

Perhaps Margaret will need this entire year to discover herself in love with Rupert, thought Mrs. Dashwood privately. *Or,* she further considered, *Margaret may discover that she is only enchanted by Rupert's work.*

In many ways, the latter was Mrs. Dashwood's biggest fear for the relationship between Margaret and Rupert. Margaret loved a project, and she longed for the life of a professor — an occupation closed to her because she was a woman. This often made Mrs. Dashwood worry that Margaret would attach herself to a gentleman for the sake of garnering some sense of purpose professionally, since Margaret could not technically have a profession. Mrs. Dashwood worried she would seek out that purpose in a mate.

Mrs. Dashwood had been thankful that her two older daughters seemed content with the future of marriage and motherhood. Elinor and Marianne had their passions, but not necessarily vocations. Mrs. Dashwood suspected that Margaret had a rather intense vocation for writing, but there was not exactly an outlet for Margaret to experiment with this desire — hence the intense relationship with Rupert.

Mrs. Dashwood, although she wished for her youngest daughter to experience love, worried that, if "a vocation" was the true reason Margaret was so attached to Rupert, then a potential marriage between the two young people would fail. It would fail because Margaret would very quickly understand that a marriage cannot simply be built upon a shared project. If Margaret wanted an intellectual marriage, she would also have to understand that intellectualism could not be constantly upheld. There must be some space to be human.

Mrs. Dashwood did not claim to be an expert on marriage, but she had felt that her experience with Mr. Dashwood had taught her some important lessons about partnership. Mr. Dashwood had been slightly older than Mrs. Dashwood, and Mrs. Dashwood was his second wife. Although Mr. Dashwood had asked his son John from his first marriage to look after his second wife and the three daughters, John Dashwood and his wife Fanny had not been particularly generous with providing for the security of the Dashwood women. This experience taught Mrs. Dashwood the reality of the precarity of marriage. When she had first married Mr. Dashwood, she had felt that she was secure for the rest of her life. As it turned out, she was not. Regardless of her husband's intentions, she and her daughters lived in a society that often neglected women through legal means.

Occasionally, Mrs. Dashwood thought mournfully that these events, which had happened when Margaret was around thirteen, had unfortunately shaped Margaret's view of marriage. All in all, Mrs. Dashwood wondered if this life experience had made Margaret resistant to marriage. But what could Mrs. Dashwood do? Their life was their life. Their experience was their experience. Yes, it had been hard, but luckily Marianne and Elinor had found good matches. And it was much easier to provide financially for a mother and one daughter than it was for a mother and *three* growing daughters.

Mrs. Dashwood felt that she understood her two older daughters. But Margaret was a bit of a mystery. Maybe this is often the case with the youngest child, but Mrs. Dashwood struggled to understand what motivated Margaret each day. She could see very clearly that Margaret did not seem overly interested in romance or the potential of motherhood, but she was at a loss for how reading and studying seemed to fill this void. Mrs. Dashwood and Margaret lived in a small village with only a handful of acquaintances. To be sure, they had the Middletons and the Jenningses to keep them company, but Margaret lacked people who were close in age to her. Mrs. Dashwood often wondered if Margaret was one of only a few twenty-eight-year-olds within a half-day's journey.

This lack of immediate friends might also account for Margaret's attachment to Rupert. He was one of the few young people with whom Margaret connected. Perhaps Mrs. Dashwood should not be surprised that Margaret and Rupert were so close.

In reality, though, Mrs. Dashwood's musings over Margaret were not entirely in vain. Margaret had *some* interest in marriage, but she was not incessantly thinking about it now. When she first came out in London ten years ago, however, it was certainly on her mind. One of the most attractive features about marriage was its promise of happiness, something that she had certainly seen in the lives of her two sisters. Margaret longed for companionship, but she knew that she was particular enough to be picky about what that companionship looked like. What she wanted most was to read great literature, especially works from the Renaissance, and try to feel her way into the work of scholarly writing. These pursuits interested her more than marriage, if she was honest. If she could not be a university professor (her secret dream, which her mother clearly perceived), she could at least attempt to write like one, if only for her own sense of confidence.

But on this particular morning while her mother questioned her once again about marriage, and especially about Rupert, Margaret stared out the window and wondered what it might be like to suddenly shift into the role of wife. She was twenty-eight, after all. If she was going to get married, she was beginning to stare down the period of time where people considered her to be at the end of her prime. It was not that she agreed with their assessment, but a small part of her began to wonder that if she did not marry now, perhaps she never would.

Out the window, she watched the leaves on the trees begin their slow process of yellowing and browning with the coming fall.

Chapter Two

The morning of Rupert's arrival in the village was filled with excitement. Margaret rose before dawn, determined to complete her own daily allotment of reading and writing before he had a chance to arrive. Margaret had already tested out how long it would take for her to walk from her cottage to the one that he was leasing. Fifteen minutes of brisk walking seemed to her the perfect distance between friends. It was just far enough that they would treasure seeing each other and just close enough that a visit could be obtained on the slightest notice.

Margaret had not seen Rupert for nearly six months. Over the summer months, he had been busy traveling. Margaret was jealous that Rupert had the ability to travel so freely. She had not yet completed her own European Tour, something that women like her often only experienced on their honeymoons if they married serviceably rich.

She was surprised to feel something akin to nervousness on this particular morning. Was she nervous about Rupert coming to live in her village for an entire year? Nonsense. This was her friend, and she had been looking forward to his sabbatical for a long while. Margaret stilled herself over her tea and paused to travel deep inside her mind to weed out the source of her anxiety. She could not see it clearly, but she had a suspicion that her nervousness had something to do with the opinions of others. Yes, this was probably the culprit. Although their neighbors were friendly, Margaret understood that these country folk would have a hard time *not* gossiping about the relationship between Margaret and Rupert. They were sure to create their own elaborate suspicions about the nature of their friendship. Margaret liked attention, but this was not the attention she preferred.

After she had taken her breakfast, completed her toilette, and finished her daily portion of writing and studying, Margaret found herself with nothing to do. Rupert was not expected until the late afternoon, so Margaret had the whole day ahead of her to sit in anticipation of her friend's arrival. Mrs. Dashwood, always curious about the state of her youngest daughter's mind, watched her listlessness with amusement. Margaret was never idle. Indeed, Margaret Dashwood was never at a loss for what to do. But waiting for the arrival of her friend to start his yearlong sabbatical had paralyzed Margaret with an overwhelming sense of frenetic anticipation.

But as she watched Margaret on the morning of Rupert's anticipated arrival, she suddenly wished that Margaret had a few more female friends. Margaret looked anxious, even though she did her best to try and assume a calm demeanor. Mrs. Dashwood could not resist prying a bit...

"Margaret, dear," asked Mrs. Dashwood, "are you quite well?"

"I am fine, Mother," said Margaret. "I just don't quite know what to do with myself."

"Your sister Marianne always found it quite helpful to fill idle time with walking," said Mrs. Dashwood. "If Rupert is not expected until later in the afternoon, then why not expel some of this nervous energy with exercise?"

Margaret got up quickly to look out the window.

"It looks as though it might rain," she said.

"Perhaps it will," said Mrs. Dashwood, "but you don't have to go far. Besides, it doesn't appear to me that you are trying to *impress* Rupert Smith, so I don't believe there is much risk in you appearing to him a touch sweaty, my dear."

Margaret gave her mother a hard look, grabbed her shawl, and walked briskly out the front door.

***

As she walked away from the cottage, Margaret took a moment to glance back and survey her home, which was now set against a darkening sky. Although it had been many years, Margaret still remembered the sensation of seeing this cottage for the first time. After the death of their father,

Margaret, her mother, and her two sisters had essentially been pushed out of their late father's home by their half brother and his wife. Margaret had been grateful to get out of the big house, even though she had plenty of happy memories there. That home only reminded her of her father, and she felt jealous of all the extra years that her older sisters had enjoyed with such a kind man.

When the Dashwood women had first arrived at the cottage, Margaret was the only one who was secretly excited. To her, the cottage looked like something out of a fairy tale, surrounded by wildflowers and ivy. It was petite, but it wasn't a hovel. It was a perfectly respectable place for the Dashwood women to live. In one of the sturdiest trees in the garden, a treehouse had been built for Margaret to play in. The treehouse looked a little dilapidated now, though. Indeed, no one had climbed up inside of it in several years. It was overgrown with ivy and moss, and Margaret suspected that it might not be able to hold the weight of a grown woman like her. But it gave her comfort to see the treehouse surveying the cottage. She had often imagined when she was younger that the treehouse was actually a crow's nest on a great ship — and that she, Margaret, was the lookout.

The image of a sailor high in a crow's nest resonated with Margaret even now. She imagined herself looking out over an expansive sea, feeling as if she were soaring over the waters. All around her was possibility. All around her was adventure. There was a degree of terror in the unknown waters, but the terror was more pleasurable than it was disconcerting. This image in her mind, however, was complicated by the fact that as soon as she looked down, she would find herself in a circular basket. In her imagination, it seemed more a cage than a basket. The image frustrated Margaret. She quickly shook her head, trying to push the picture out of her mind, and she began to walk toward the moors that surrounded the cottage.

She compelled herself to walk quickly, trying to make her legs burn with energy. She considered that a little bit of discomfort might take her mind off the events of the day. Her conversation with her mother had made her wonder if she had not put enough time into thinking realistically about the structure of the coming year. She had anticipated that she would see Rupert on an almost daily basis in order to help him work, but her mother's questions gave her reservations. What if Rupert did not wish to see her every day? What if he only wanted an editor and not a collaborator? In their letters, he always seemed so receptive to her ideas, but Margaret was unsure if that epistolary enthusiasm would transpose to an in-person scholarly partnership.

She comforted herself by thinking about her ideas. Rupert wished to write about Shakespeare's history plays, but Margaret hoped to convince him to focus on the often forgotten *female* characters of the history plays. These female characters rarely got attention. When people attempted to have thoughtful discussions about these plays, the women were nearly always forgotten, even though most of the ones who appeared in the history plays were royalty. Her great fear was that Rupert would be convinced that a book on the history plays that only considered male characters would be sufficient. If this was what he believed, Margaret felt that he could not be more wrong.

Rupert usually listened to her, though, and she smiled when she thought back over the ten-year history of their friendship. When Margaret had first met Rupert, he had seemed barely out of childhood. Upon reflection, Margaret understood that she had probably seemed the same way to him. In ten years' time, both Margaret and Rupert had grown in their intelligence, their empathy, and their sense of purpose. If Margaret was honest with herself, she could not imagine a life without Rupert. Her mother had raised the question of love enough that Margaret occasionally doubted her conviction that she and Rupert were merely friends.

In truth, Margaret was experiencing one of those moments of doubt right now.

She stood on the highest point of a moor and pretended once again that she was in the crow's nest of a ship. Instead of the ocean all around her, she was surrounded by green grass that would soon turn stiff and brownish with the coming fall.

She stretched her arms upward and felt her rib cage lift and expand. On her tiptoes, she reached for the sky and wished that the sun were out to kiss her fingertips with warmth. She did her best to make herself taller so that she could see herself as a giant on top of the moor. Margaret was on the small side, but when she stood at a high elevation with her arms outstretched and her toes straining with the weight of her body, then she got to experience that brief moment of feeling large and expansive. It made her feel powerful. It made her feel that maybe she wasn't trapped inside this small woman's body. It made her feel that the moors, the sky, and the lack of people all around her made it so that her size and her femaleness did not matter. It was the best of feelings, and it was exactly what she needed on this morning of strange anxiety.

If Margaret questioned herself frankly, she knew exactly what was on her mind. Nearly a year ago, while visiting family in London, Margaret and Rupert had spent several weeks enjoying one another's company in the city. They had attended plays and concerts, and they had enjoyed daily walks around the city, arm in arm. After so many years, most of their acquaintances had ceased to wonder if Margaret and Rupert would ever marry. Only Mrs. Dashwood kept that flame burning. But those weeks in London had branded themselves into Margaret's mind as an idyllic and wonderful season. Their friendship had never been stronger, and the books and conversations they shared only confirmed their joint enthusiasm for studying great literature. They also benefited from a shared history that made their friendship all the more rich.

But those wonderful weeks had ended on a sour note. On one of the final nights that Margaret was in London, she and Rupert had shared an odd conversation, one that she simply could not forget.

The conversation happened thus:

"Margaret," Rupert began (the two of them had long ago tossed aside the formalities of "Miss" and "Professor"). "Margaret, you and I are good at theorizing about everything, don't you think?"

"Oh, indeed," said Margaret, laughing. "We are the finest."

"Let's have a drink and spend our last evening here theorizing," he said. "What do you say?"

"I say order me some champagne and toss me a concept, my friend," said a playful Margaret.

They sat together at a small outdoor table at a fine restaurant. Rupert ordered a flute of champagne for Margaret and a whiskey for himself. Before the theorizing commenced, they clinked their drinks in friendship.

"Margaret, I know we never speak of marriage, but I wonder if you've had any space privately in your mind to consider your own philosophy of matrimony." He took a quick sip of his drink and attempted to read her expression.

"A philosophy of *marriage*?" asked Margaret. "What do you mean by that, Rupert?"

"I mean that, if you were a philosopher, what would you say the purpose of marriage truly is?"

"Are you thinking of getting married, Rupert?" teased Margaret.

"That's not what I asked, my friend," he said.

"Ah, I see," said Margaret, "you need my philosophical advice before you can come around to developing your own opinion on the subject."

He smiled. "Yes, that's exactly it, Margaret."

Margaret thought for a moment. Did she even have a philosophy of marriage? She had certainly watched her older sisters find great satisfaction in their marriages, but she didn't really know what the daily happenings of those marriages were. What did her sisters *do* all day as married women? To be sure, they had young children that they cared for, but her sisters also had the help of a hired staff to wrangle the little ones. Margaret assumed that their marriages were filled with conversation, but she was unsure what they spent their time talking about. She knew without a doubt that Marianne and Elinor loved their husbands deeply — this one aspect of their marriages was absolutely true.

But if love was the only element of marriage that Margaret could be sure of, then she was still at a loss. Margaret was quite sure that she had never been in love. As a young woman, she had never felt the overwhelming sensation of attraction to another human. As someone who was always in motion, she certainly did not have time to pine for a beloved. Margaret did not know what it was like for her thoughts to be consumed with another person. Did this make her self-centered? She was not sure. However, she *was* sure that the love her sisters felt for their husbands was the real thing. Margaret understood that love was a true phenomenon that existed, but it pained her to realize that she had never enjoyed it.

Except... there was one time, back when the Dashwood women had first moved into the cottage after the death of Mr. Dashwood. There was a gentleman who briefly courted Marianne that Margaret had never forgotten. He was a rogue, though, who ultimately broke her sister's heart. Mr. John Willoughby, the cavalier in question, had left Marianne in pursuit of a wealthier match. Margaret knew that it was her duty as Marianne's sister to hate Willoughby, but when Margaret had only been thirteen and Willoughby had been one of the first gentlemen she had ever encountered, she had thought him the *finest* man in the world. When Margaret reflected on that season now, it occurred to her that the brief infatuation she felt for Willoughby was perhaps the closest she had ever inched toward romantic love.

With all of these thoughts pressing on her mind, Margaret finally answered Rupert's question about a philosophy of marriage.

"I do not claim to know much of love," began Margaret, "but I am of the opinion that money and wealth are secondary concerns in matrimony. My sisters married for great love, and issues of money were the only things that caused problems in their pursuit of happiness."

"That's all well and good," interrupted Rupert, "but, Margaret, what do you believe marriage is *for*?"

Margaret smiled. "If I were a character in a book and another character asked me such a question, I would say, 'The purpose of marriage is to exist in communion with another person who helps you become a grander and more wonderful version of yourself.' But, as I am not a character in a novel, I must confess that I don't know if such a process is real. I like to believe that it is, but everything in my rational mind tells me that this is too idealistic."

Rupert sipped his drink. "But Margaret, how then do you distinguish your philosophy of marriage from genuine friendship? What is the line between friends and lovers?"

"I suppose if two people truly wish to be lovers," said Margaret, "then they would be *incapable* of resisting the urge to consummate such love. Friends who are destined to remain friends will do so — a lover cannot help being a lover. Romance and love are inevitable when you find yourself a lover, I think. I am not saying that such a state guarantees a happy ending, but it at least ensures action."

Rupert was silent for a moment. "I think you are right," he said slowly. "If the action is inevitable, then it would have happened long ago."

He then finished his drink and told Margaret that he had an early morning. He left a bit of money for her to pay the bill. And then he disappeared into the London night.

That was the last time Margaret had seen Rupert. It had been several months now since that moment, and although they had exchanged many letters in the interim, the fact that their last in person meeting had ended so strangely filled Margaret with an unfamiliar anxiety at seeing him once more.

In their letters over the past months, Rupert never alluded to their conversation at the café. His letters had been all business. He offered ideas for his book project, asked for suggestions about some of those ideas, and inquired about her health and that of her mother. If Margaret was candid with herself, she could concede that Rupert's tone had changed. Margaret had long thought that their ten-year friendship had finally passed the threshold of staying as friends forever, but their last conversation made her wonder if Rupert had begun to change his mind. Of course, Margaret never once mentioned any of these suspicions to Mrs. Dashwood. Margaret kept this information very much to herself.

But the surge of anxiety that she was feeling on the moors today made her feel that she ought to give some consideration to the relationship between herself and Rupert. He would be living in her immediate vicinity for an entire year. They had never before spent so much time within walking distance of one another. How would their relationship change? Margaret decided to be practical for a moment, something that she did not always do naturally.

She thought to herself, *What if I spent the next year evaluating whether or not I could be, or already am, in love with Rupert Smith?* It surprised her that this question came to her mind, but it was an eminently practical idea. It would be a good idea to spend the next year conducting a kind of romantic experiment in which she attempted to perceive her own affections. For someone who wasn't sure if she had ever been in love, aside from her youthful infatuation with Mr. Willoughby, a scientific experiment might ease her mind.

While pacing at the top of a moor between two small trees, Margaret considered her methodology for this experiment:

Number one: Whenever she was in the presence of Rupert, her intention was to maintain sustained eye contact with him in order to perceive if this aroused emotions within her. She had read enough novels to understand that eye contact meant *something*, so she thought she might as well test out the theory.

Number two: She would endeavor to speak about topics with Rupert that were more personal, perhaps even more relationship-minded. Their conversations frequently centered upon literature and philosophy, but it might be nice to better know the inner workings of his mind. Perhaps a little bit of emotional intimacy would fan the flames of potential love?

Number three: If Rupert hinted at something akin to romance, Margaret resolved not to shut it down, but instead to follow her interest and listen deep within herself to her response. She had a tendency to be evasive when it came to matters of romantic attachments, but she decided that, with Rupert, she would pay attention. Maybe this kind of attention would cause her to respond.

And number four: If, after a year's time, Margaret felt that she could not bear being separated from Rupert and her previous experiments had given pleasure and satisfaction, then she would bring up the conversation of marriage herself. Of course, this went against all forms of propriety and social convention, but Margaret felt that she was on good enough terms with Rupert to raise the subject.

There was one small caveat to her methodology, however. Margaret did not allow herself to consider what the outcome might be if Rupert explicitly claimed that he *did not wish* to consider marriage with her. She decided she would cross that bridge when she got to it. For now, she must focus on her experiment.

Just as she felt a wave of resolve wash over her, Margaret heard a low rumble from the clouds in the distance, and then the raindrops began to fall. At first they were scanty, but then the rain-drops fell in large torrents that began to soak her hair down to her scalp. Margaret had known something like this might happen, so she was not too worried. She was sure she would have plenty of time to return to the cottage and clean up before Rupert arrived. The walk had been just what she needed, and she felt herself continuing to expel all of her nervous energy as she walked quickly in the rain back toward her home.

She had not intended to stray too far from the cottage, but her wandering mind had guided her wandering feet to a considerable length away from home. By the time she arrived at the front gate, her skirts were soaked with mud, her hair was sopping, and her skin was glistening with droplets. She looked like a wild woman, but Margaret considered that she was often only a few steps from being a wild woman on any given day. The rain pounded even harder and so Margaret ran up the final stretch of the small hill on which the house was built.

She burst into the front door and immediately yelled out, "Well, Mother, I was right about the rain! An absolute downpour! Thank goodness Rupert isn't arriving until later!"

Just as Margaret was finishing her sentence, she turned and faced the parlor. Before her were three figures: one was Mrs. Dashwood, the other was a young woman she did not recognize (although Mrs. Dashwood often entertained callers that Margaret did not know), and, standing by the fireplace, was *him*.

It was Rupert, dressed like a gentleman and not at all hiding his shock at seeing Margaret soaked to the bone. Margaret immediately felt her "experiment" begin working. He seemed to her completely different from the last time they had been together. He appeared more at ease with his body, more relaxed in his overall presentation. Margaret was surprised at how her heart immediately warmed to seeing him in her own home, and Margaret loved being surprised.

Margaret did not waste a moment in greeting him. Not caring how she looked, she slopped her way into the sitting room, treading mud behind her, and enveloped Rupert in a soggy embrace.

"Oh, Rupert!" she said. "You're early! Look at the *state* I'm in! But no matter. Give me only a moment, and I'll be down so that we can begin our yearlong adventure." She squeezed his shoulders and laughed with delight. "It gives me so much joy for you to be here, dear friend," she said.

But Rupert's body felt stiff in Margaret's wet embrace, the opposite of what she expected when she found herself attracted to his new aura of ease. Something was the matter. She was not quite sure what the problem was, but something had clearly changed.

Margaret backed away slightly so that she could get a better look at his face.

"Rupert, is everything alright? I'm sorry if I've soaked your clothes. I was just too excited." She added, "Is something wrong?"

Gently, though decidedly, Rupert pushed Margaret a little away from him and then reached his arm out to the young woman whom Margaret had already forgotten.

"Miss Margaret, I do not wish to deprive you any longer of the pleasure of meeting my new wife," said Rupert. "Please allow me the honor of introducing to you Mrs. Cecelia Smith, my wife of three weeks."

Margaret froze. The only sound in the sitting room was the steady dripping of the water from the bottom of her skirts. Forcing her mouth into something like a smile, Margaret turned her body toward the young woman in front of her, the one she had so easily ignored. Cecelia Smith looked to be no more than twenty years old, and she had the face of a cherub. Looking at the young woman more closely, Margaret was surprised that she had not noticed Cecelia's beauty immediately. Cecelia Smith seemed to shine. Indeed, she appeared to be the brightest light in the small sitting room.

"My dear Miss Margaret," Cecelia chirped in a birdlike voice. "I am so happy to finally make your acquaintance. The professor speaks so highly of you, and I do hope that we will become great friends!"

"*The professor*," thought Margaret. *So that is what we are to call him now.*

"Yes, indeed!" said Margaret. She was so entranced by the beautiful voice of Cecelia, Rupert's *wife*, that she did not have time to assess all of the feelings she was experiencing internally.

She shot a glance in Rupert's direction, as if to say secretly, *Why did you say nothing of this?*

She turned her attention back to Cecelia and felt herself falling deep into a swift comparison of herself to the charming young woman before her. Cecelia Smith could not be more different from Margaret Dashwood. Margaret understood this difference within seconds of making this young woman's acquaintance. It was not so much a difference in physical appearance, although Cecelia seemed to be much more waifish and fairylike than the strongly built Margaret; it was more a difference in energy. Cecelia emanated an energy of softness and grace that Margaret had little sense of how to emulate. Margaret, for her part, generally vibrated with great intensity, an intensity that felt overwhelming and possibly catastrophic when confronted with sweet Cecelia.

Propriety took over, though, and Margaret spoke: "My dear Mrs. Smith, I am so glad to meet you. Please accept my apologies for my current state! The storm stumbled upon me completely unaware. If you will wait just a few moments, I will return clean and dry so that we can officially commence our friendship."

Cecelia beamed and made a kind of squeaking sound to show her excitement. Margaret attempted to squeak back, but it came out more as a light grunt.

Margaret turned to go upstairs, but before she left the sitting room, she looked blankly at Rupert. She was not sure how to convey with her eyes the mixture of emotions that she was feeling. If it was something like happiness, she could only show blankness. And if it was something like pain, her face only revealed indifference.

She left the room standing tall, but she had to pause and steady herself as soon as she turned the corner.

Chapter Three

Margaret looked at herself in her bedroom mirror. She looked horrible, but it wasn't just her soaked clothes and her muddy petticoats that contributed to such an effect. The expression on her face was what really set the tone for her appearance. In the future, Margaret would come to describe it as a look of shock, but in this moment it only looked like emptiness.

Margaret usually loved surprises, especially when those surprises were just for her, but this was not the surprise she had been expecting. In only a few months' time, Rupert had apparently met, courted, and *married* this young woman, all without even mentioning that fact to Margaret. And Margaret had thought that she was Rupert's dearest friend! Why would he withhold this vital information from her?

Truth be told, Margaret was hurt. As she stared at herself in the mirror, it became even more clear to her that Rupert had intentionally kept the relationship secret. He must have stayed silent on the subject for fear of how Margaret might respond. It occurred to Margaret that his fears were probably warranted.

Although Margaret and Rupert had not often spoken of love and courtship in their long friendship, Margaret had wasted a fair amount of breath deriding the marriage-obsessed culture of her fellow young women. Margaret fancied herself high above this obsession, and she loved to poke fun at the silly girls who frequented the London balls in constant pursuit of a husband. Margaret had been brutal in her assessment of these women's singular focus on marriage. And Cecelia, in fact, was *exactly* the type of woman that Margaret would be quick to deride.

As she pulled off her wet clothes, her nakedness reminded her of the shame she now felt. She knew that Rupert had listened to all of her jibes and that these were certainly in his mind when he chose Cecelia as his wife.

How could she have been so cruel? Cecelia seemed like a perfectly nice girl, and yet Margaret had spent such a long time denigrating her caste of marriageable ladies. Had Rupert told Cecelia of Margaret's words? This thought introduced a new fear: how much had Rupert told Cecelia about Margaret in general? Cecelia had expressed a keen interest to begin a friendship with Margaret, but upon what basis was that desire founded?

Margaret was not sure. She realized that there was nothing she was sure about at this moment. The terms of her relationship with Rupert had changed irrevocably. He was *married* now.

Everything would be different — of this Margaret was sure.

All the plans she had devised on the hillside felt trivial to her now. Her strange plan of developing an experiment in love was useless in the face of the beautiful Mrs. Cecelia Smith. And she *was* beautiful, like some sort of fairy tale creature. This was one fact that alarmed Margaret deeply, for reasons she could not fully understand. After a moment, Margaret realized the element of Mrs. Smith's existence that bothered her: not only was she beautiful, but she also seemed to be significantly younger than Margaret.

Margaret had always been happy with whatever age she was, and she quite liked age twenty-eight. But the youth and beauty of Mrs. Smith made her feel *off* — she was not used to feeling this compulsion toward comparison, and yet she was feeling it now in full force.

Margaret found herself investigating her wardrobe with an eye toward her more youthful day dresses, but this impulse disgusted her. Why did she need to "feel" younger in the presence of Mrs. Smith? Margaret was the age that she was. There was nothing to be done about it. But the fact that Mrs. Smith was married (to *Rupert*, of all people) made Margaret at least feel a difference in *experience*. Margaret, of course, had never been married; there was a whole element of human existence, particularly in the physical realm, that she had no knowledge of. But Cecelia Smith evidently knew all by this point. Margaret struggled when people had access to knowledge that she did not, especially when it was another woman.

She chose a modest blue gown and did the best she could with her soggy hair. There was very little to be done to make her look any more put together than she could presently manage. She looked the way she looked, and she must accept it. But Margaret implicitly understood that this impulse to suddenly take a bit more care with her appearance was connected to a desire to grab Rupert's attention. Although it felt odd to acknowledge this fact, albeit inwardly, she felt a pang in her heart when she remembered swiftly that Rupert was *married*.

It was time for Margaret to go back downstairs. She had done the best she could with her appearance, but it really didn't matter. Who was there to impress? Rupert was married, and if Margaret ever had doubts about her relationship with Rupert being one of friendship, those doubts were dissolved now. He was a married man, and she needed to treat him as such. She wondered if she would feel comfortable referring to him as "professor." It only took a few seconds of reflection for her to realize that this one change, at least, would not be possible for her. Rupert would forever be *Rupert*. Hopefully this one quirk would not upset Cecelia Smith too much.

Before entering the sitting room, Margaret stood around the corner and listened to the conversation. Interestingly, Cecelia was the voice that seemed to be leading the discourse. Margaret realized very quickly that Cecelia was used to being the center of attention, and she held that attention quite well. Like most cultured young ladies, Cecelia knew how to carry on a lively conversation with just about anyone, and Margaret could tell that she was hard at work to create a memorable chatty moment in the Dashwoods' parlor.

"When the dear professor told me that we would be spending his sabbatical in the countryside, I was overcome with excitement," said Cecelia's melodic voice. "After the flurry of our engagement and wedding, I was so eager to get out of the city and back into the fresh air of the country! We need some open space in order to get acquainted with one another, don't we, my dear?" Cecelia unleashed a charming giggle.

"Yes," said Rupert, "I was a little nervous that Mrs. Smith would not be amenable to a sabbatical in the countryside, but I suppose I shouldn't be surprised. The nature of my relationship to Mrs. Smith has been nothing but surprises since we first met."

Inwardly, Margaret groaned, although she didn't dare let the sound escape her body. Who was this man, suddenly so enraptured with marriage to this birdlike woman? She hardly recognized her friend. Instead of feeling hurt that he had not disclosed his marriage to her, Margaret began to feel a sense of indignation at the strange, altered friend who stood in the parlor, hovering over his charming little wife.

Margaret turned the corner and wasted no time announcing herself.

"Well," she said, "I have made myself as presentable as possible and I hope you will forgive it." Margaret walked to the fireplace and quickly positioned herself between Rupert and Cecelia, focusing as much of her attention as she could muster on the little woman. Margaret was not particularly tall, but she found herself towering over the tiny Cecelia. This difference in height gave Margaret a small touch of confidence, and she decided to capitalize on it.

"Now, Mrs. Smith," said Margaret, "you must tell me the whole history of your relationship with our dear Rupert. You see, he has been so busy preparing for this sabbatical that he is not taken the time to *mention* you, which communicates to me that you, my dear, must be the one to tell us the story in full."

Cecelia looked mildly alarmed. She glanced at Rupert and said in a small voice, "My dear, did you not tell them that we were married?"

Rupert only said with calmness, "I hoped to make it a surprise."

Whatever concerns Cecelia might have had over Rupert's lack of disclosure dissipated. Margaret could tell that Cecelia loved being the secret surprise.

"Oh, my darling, you are such a trickster,"

squeaked Cecelia.

"That he is," added Margaret. "Now, my dear, please tell us everything." Margaret's eyes shifted to Rupert's as if to say, *If you will tell me nothing, this little bird woman will.*

Everyone sat comfortably in the parlor and turned their attention to the beautiful Mrs. Cecelia Smith as she began to tell the whole history of her marriage to Professor Rupert Smith.

All in all, it was not a terribly unique story, but the way Cecelia told it made one think that it was (to her) the greatest romance of all time. Cecelia was the daughter of one of Rupert's senior colleagues at the university. Her father was a respected member of the classics faculty and had taken an interest in Rupert as a junior scholar. Because Rupert was well-versed in Latin, this senior colleague had asked Rupert to attend to his youngest daughter, who was endeavoring to get better at Latin as one of her accomplishments. Rupert, for his part, had been understandably intrigued by a young woman interested in Latin. Most young ladies had accomplishments such as drawing, piano playing, singing, or harp playing — but Latin was unusual.

Cecelia giggled unceasingly when she reached the part of the story where Rupert made his first visit to her family's home in London. There had been talk all week of a new young professor coming to dinner to offer some instruction to Cecelia. What Rupert had not realized was that Cecelia's Latin was no better than that of a child who had barely finished grammar school. Her interest in Latin was merely a party trick, not a scholarly endeavor. Cecelia laughed as she recounted her realization that Rupert expected her to be a much better scholar than she actually was, but their laughter over her poor Latin turned toward conversation.

Rupert eventually interrupted Cecelia's storytelling so that he could give his own account.

"Meeting Cecelia was so refreshing to me," he began. "Every day, I am entrenched in academic rigor. I am constantly doing the work of teaching young students and endeavoring to hold them to the highest standard. When I met Cecelia, I was faced with the realization that academic rigor was not all that mattered. We were suddenly able to *laugh* over something as serious as Latin. My dear Cecila made me relax, and, in making me relax, she helped me fall in love."

Their courtship had been swift. Rupert was in a strong position to take a wife. He had received tenure at the university and was leasing a stylish apartment not far from his office. He was a young man of means, and he was also a working gentleman, something quite different from all of the wealthy young men who had frequented Cecelia's dance card.

Margaret was able to perceive quite quickly why Rupert might have been taken with Cecelia. Even though Cecelia was not a scholar herself, she understood the culture of university faculty members, and she knew just enough about high culture to engage with Rupert on many different subjects. But she also knew just little enough for him to still play the role of teacher in their relationship.

Cecelia appeared to be a young woman who had spent her life learning to be pleasant and joyful, a perfect picture of a lovely young woman; Margaret had also spent a large portion of her adult life learning to be pleasant and joyful, while also balancing a desire to show herself to the world as a woman who could be a respectable intellectual. This meant that Margaret did not often have the same level of immediate warmth as a woman like Cecelia because she was preoccupied with being taken seriously. She did not begrudge the presence of this warmth in Rupert's new wife. She only noted its existence.

As Margaret thought about the coming year, she became increasingly more aware of the reality that any time spent working with Rupert would be quite limited. There was now a whole other person to deal with, and Margaret had little sense of how much Cecelia wished to be involved with Rupert's sabbatical project. Margaret felt a strong desire to find answers to these questions quickly, mainly because she didn't want to waste any more of her precious energy on the anxiety of whether she would be permitted to help Rupert in the first place.

She might need to get him alone, but it struck Margaret that this was perhaps a more difficult task than it used to be. Now there was the issue of Mrs. Cecelia Smith, and Cecelia did not seem like she wanted to be any more than two feet away from Rupert at any given time. Margaret was so used to having Rupert's attention all to herself, even if they were only friends. She felt a pang of frustration when she realized that his attention was now divided, and then it occurred to her that Cecelia might even have reservations about Margaret. How welcome would Margaret be at the home of Rupert and Cecelia? Was all of this friendliness just a ruse?

Margaret stared at Cecelia and tried to perceive how genuine this young woman might be. But, looking at her beautiful face, Margaret could not detect even the slightest hint of guile. It seemed that Cecelia Smith was an angel among women, and all she really wanted was a friend. Margaret realized that she would probably have to be that friend.

After a bit more jovial discussion about the meeting of Cecelia and Rupert, Cecelia finally told the story of Rupert's proposal:

"Oh, Miss Margaret and Mrs. Dashwood, it was terribly romantic!" said Cecelia. "Rupert and I were walking home from a concert when a horrid summer storm threatened to overtake us. We had no umbrella, so we found ourselves drenched, just like you were today, Miss Margaret. We were so joyfully in love, though, that there was no way a downpour could lessen our mood. I remember saying to the professor, 'I ought to be miserable, but I must confess I am nothing but happy.' And he turned to me, his wet hair flat against his forehead, and asked, 'Do you believe there is a world in which I could make you happier, dear Cecelia?' He did not even have to ask me if I would be his wife! I simply knew and understood, and in two weeks we were married at one of the university chapels! It was a quaint affair, but perfect for the wife of a professor."

"Yes," said Mrs. Dashwood, "this all sounds remarkably romantic. Don't you think so, Margaret?"

Margaret's eyes grew wide at being prompted by her mother. "Oh, yes," she lied, "quite romantic."

Margaret understood why the story was so "perfect" to Cecelia. It had all the trappings of the climax of a courtship novel. The abandon of walking in the rain, the joyfulness, and the line about "happiness" — all of these were elements of a good conclusion to a story of pining. Margaret could tell that the appearance of Rupert in Cecelia's life had been a genuine surprise. Before he and Cecelia met, Margaret was sure that Cecelia planned to marry a wealthy gentleman who did not have to work. She was beautiful enough to have her pick of the lot, but she had chosen Rupert.

Why the devil had she chosen Rupert?

This question made Margaret consider the viability of Rupert himself as an attractive gentleman. When she and Rupert had first met over a decade ago, he had been boyish and spindly — not at all dashing. But ten years had given him a suave charisma that manifested both in his demeanor and his appearance. Margaret was barely able to admit it to herself, but he was undeniably handsome.

The visit coming to its natural end, Rupert and Cecelia said that they must get back to the home that they were renting in order to unpack and settle in, but they hoped heartily that the Dashwood women would dine with them the following night. Mrs. Dashwood and Margaret, of course, accepted the invitation. Margaret, however, was still a little confused about the role that she would be playing in Rupert's sabbatical. Did he still want her help with his book? Truly, did he want anything to do with Margaret now that he was married? Margaret did not know the best way to get this information without seeming as if she were overstepping her bounds. She had been able to put off the constraints of propriety with Rupert, but she was not sure how well she could do the same with Mrs. Cecelia Smith.

So Margaret said the diplomatic thing: "I so look forward to dining with both of you tomorrow," she began, "and, Rupert," — she turned to him — "I hope you will think hard about how I can be most helpful to you as a friend and fellow scholar while you begin your book project."

"Yes," said Rupert, "I have given the matter

a great deal of thought, and I deeply desire your help, Miss Margaret, with the project." He paused before continuing. "But I also intend to involve Mrs. Smith in the process, as well. She would like to know a bit more about my work, and I wonder if the three of us might get along well together."

"Oh, yes!" beamed Cecelia. "I so *desperately* want to know more about these dusty old books that Rupert is obsessed with! Of all of Shakespeare's plays, he likes the history plays best. Can you believe it? I cannot understand it, but as I am now Mrs. Smith I intend to try and understand it as best as I am able."

"That is very good of you," said Margaret, her eyebrows slightly raised. "I'm sure we will all learn a great deal while working together." Margaret did not necessarily mean what she had just said, but she said it anyway just to appease Cecelia and end the conversation as quickly as possible.

As Mrs. Dashwood and Margaret escorted the Smiths to the door, the rain now gone, Cecelia added one more thing. "I hope you won't mind, but a cousin of mine lives in the area and he will be bringing himself and his daughter to dine with us tomorrow!"

"As we now consider you family, Mrs. Smith, we will consider him family, as well," said Margaret, continuing her diplomatic streak.

Cecelia gave one of her signature squeaks and squeezed Margaret's hand lovingly. Margaret felt a sour taste in her mouth as she watched Rupert and Cecelia walk down the hill, framed by a shining blue sky.

Margaret could feel her mother's eyes on her back as she watched the couple descend into the now clear day. She wondered what her mother was thinking. Did she pity Margaret? Did she feel relieved that the issue of a marriage between Margaret and Rupert was now impossible? What was Mrs. Dashwood thinking?

"My darling," Margaret heard Mrs. Dashwood say. "I feel I must inquire after the state of your heart."

It was an honest and open question, and it was perhaps exactly the kind of question that Margaret needed to be asked at this moment. How *was* the state of her heart? After all, the concerns of her heart were not just connected to romance. Rupert was a dear friend, and his life was now irrevocably changed. Margaret felt her face get hot and the beginnings of tears started to burn under her eyelids. She was confused and so she only knew one way to answer her mother.

"Mother," said Margaret, "whatever the state of my heart is, I am too overwhelmed with a strange shock to see it clearly."

Mrs. Dashwood nodded. "I believe we need a little tea, perhaps something stronger," she said.

Margaret closed the front door and wandered back into the sitting room where she had first seen Rupert and Cecelia standing next to each other — so glorious and happy in their newfound matrimony. How could she be angry at Rupert when everything in his life suddenly seemed so beautiful? She admitted to herself that she could not be angry with him.

But how was she to be a friend to him during this time? Very often in these sorts of relations, the women are the ones who have the strongest friendship ties, but this was an unusual situation. Margaret and Rupert were intimate friends, although they had never been romantic with one another. Their friendship was quite sound. How would the friendship continue in such a way that genuinely accepted Cecelia as part of the company? Margaret felt deep inside that this would be a struggle she had never before encountered. She did not have many friends; indeed, Rupert was essentially at the top of her list of comrades. Now, she supposed, she would have to also add Cecelia to that list, although she did so cautiously.

When a person only has a few friends (which, in truth, is often all a human really needs), they will take great pains to protect and care for those friendships. Margaret believed she was a good friend to Rupert, and she believed that he would not throw her aside in favor of a wife. But she understood that Cecelia now gave something to Rupert that Margaret could not, under the present circumstances, ever give.

Mrs. Dashwood returned to the sitting room carrying a tray of tea that had been enriched by a bit of Scottish whisky.

"The spirits will help you keep from catching cold," said Mrs. Dashwood.

"Perhaps it will also help me think clearly," said Margaret.

Mrs. Dashwood and Margaret sat side by side on the tufted couch that had been in their family for over a decade. This little couch, which comfortably only sat two people, had been one of their first purchases when they moved into the cottage all those years ago. At the time, it had seemed like quite a fine piece of furniture. Now it was weathered. Perhaps it was weathered not only from all of the traffic that went in and out of the sitting room, but also the painful scenes of love that it had witnessed (and maybe some of the joy, too). In this room, Mr. Willoughby had first brought Marianne home after rescuing her from a twisted ankle on the moors. This room had also seen the conversation between the two of them that resulted in Mr. Willoughby leaving her forever. More charmingly, this was the room in which Edward Ferrars finally proposed to Elinor. *Oh, what this room has seen!* thought Margaret. Now she could add herself to the list of events that had taken place in the small room. She had not exactly had her heart broken in here, but she had experienced a sensation of great intensity, a feeling that she could not name.

Only when she stilled herself was she able to admit that it might just be profound grief.

Chapter Four

The next morning, Margaret took herself on one of her regular walks. She decided to skip her daily allotment of reading and studying. She was too frustrated by the new situation with Rupert to think about her work at present. All she could do now was walk. So, she trudged through the dew-soaked grass in the cool, early fall air and made her way to one of her favorite thinking spots.

On the crest of a nearby hill was a kind of ruin — an odd assortment of large boulders that gave the impression of being intentionally placed there. Margaret had spent much of her late adolescence making up stories about these stones: They could be a meeting place, a sacrificial altar, or perhaps a magical conjuring spot. But today, the stones were a comfort.

Margaret had barely slept the night before. Instead, she had used the darkness of her bedroom as a means of diving deep into her mind in order to discover what she was feeling. She did not have an abundance of clear answers, but she had a good sense of what she felt. A restless night staring into the darkness can give a person a surprising amount of clarity. What she had learned was this: for nearly ten years, Margaret had felt a kind of ownership over Rupert, an ownership that she was not at all entitled to. In fact, this sense of ownership went against many of Margaret's own principles for equality among human beings. Upon further reflection, she thought how ridiculous it was that she felt that she "owned" Rupert.

She had no claim over him, no reason to think that he was wholly devoted to her in his friendship. If Rupert was married, it must be because he *wanted* to be married. He was certainly not forced into making such a decision, and Margaret must accept his autonomy. Although she wished that he had given her warning about Mrs. Cecelia Smith, she understood that she was not owed any explanation at all. If he did not wish to tell her, he did not have to tell her. The fact that he was telling her now was one of absolute necessity.

But the feeling of grief she had experienced the night before still weighed on her heavily. She was in mourning for the loss of a friendship with Rupert as it was before. That friendship would never quite be the same again. She felt sad, but there was nothing to be done except meet Rupert where he was.

Sitting atop one of the stones, Margaret sensed that she was no longer alone. She turned and saw a gentleman in a long coat making his way in her direction. She knew the silhouette instantly:

It was Rupert, and he was alone. In the few moments before he made it to the top of the hill where Margaret was perched, she resolved to be friendly, to not shame him for telling her nothing of Cecelia, and, above all, to show that she cared.

"Good morning, Rupert," said Margaret cheerfully. "I see you are deciding whether or not a morning walk on the moors will be part of your sabbatical ritual," she added, smiling.

At first, Rupert said nothing. He only stood at a slight distance and half smiled at his friend.

"I'm sorry I didn't tell you," he said eventually. "You are my friend, but I was afraid you would judge me. Indeed, I believe you have judged me already," he said.

"Rupert, I *am* surprised," said Margaret, "but I do not intend to judge you for your decisions."

"Margaret, I know you well enough to know that you are incapable of withholding judgment, especially for me," he said.

Margaret blushed a little. He was not wrong.

"Well," she said, "if I feel compelled to judge, it is not my business to share it with you. That would be rude. I am resolved *not* to be rude, especially to your darling Mrs. Smith."

"Ah, see," he said, "but there it is: 'my darling' Mrs. Smith."

"Is that not what she is?" said Margaret playfully.

Rupert became serious. "Margaret, I need you to understand that Cecelia *is* darling to me. She is my wife. Please, I beg of you, do not tease me for my decision. I have yearned for love for a long time, and in Cecelia I have found a joyful partner. Please, allow me that indulgence, even if you find her silly."

"Or young," interrupted Margaret.

Rupert laughed. "You know as well as I do that nearly all the women who seek marriage are younger than me ... and you," he added.

"Rupert, I had no idea you were interested in getting married, at least not now," said Margaret. "I suppose that's not something you ever needed to tell me, my friend, but it would have been nice to be prepared for this."

"Why?" said Rupert. "Does it bother you that I am a married man now?"

Margaret thought about his question. How could she answer honestly? Would it hurt him if she told him the truth? Would he ever trust her again?

"It does not bother me that you are married, Rupert," she said. "The only thing that troubles me is that I don't know how to continue our friendship in the way that it was. It must be different now that Mrs. Cecelia Smith is a reality. I am also not fully convinced that you want my help with your book. I confess, I had plans that we would eventually end up writing something as coauthors, but now I feel that such an endeavor would lack all propriety. And, Rupert, I am not sure how well I will work with your Mrs. Smith. I am also unconvinced that it is partially my responsibility to help her understand what it is you study." Margaret said this last bit pointedly.

She continued further: "I do wish you would tell me some of what you have already communicated to Cecelia about our friendship with one another. It is unconventional for a man and a woman to be friends such as we are. People have whispered about us before. Now that you are married, the danger of those whispers increases dramatically. You do see that, don't you, Rupert?"

"Yes, of course I see that," cut in Rupert. "And as for what I have told Cecelia of you, I have only been honest. She knows that we are close. She knows that we have never been romantically involved, and she knows that the one force that unites us the most is our scholarship. I cannot speak for Cecelia herself, but I do not believe she is jealous of you. I don't think she ever will be jealous of you."

For some reason, this comment stung. Practically speaking, it was good to hear that Rupert believed Cecelia would not harbor any animosity towards Margaret, but in terms of Margaret's ego, this comment hurt quite a lot. Margaret liked to be admired. She liked for people to be impressed by her. In truth, she did not mind when they were jealous of her and her personality. But Rupert's dismissal of any possibility of Mrs. Cecelia Smith being jealous of Margaret and her connection to Rupert made Margaret feel strange.

The most experience Margaret had with the secret thoughts of other women was by way of her older sisters. Those two relationships had taught her that jealousy among women was almost as natural as breathing. Margaret felt sure that, even if Cecelia were not jealous now, she might be jealous in the future, and Margaret felt that it was her duty to defer that possibility for as long as she could.

"Rupert," said Margaret, "do you truly want my help with your book? You know I am eager to help, but I do not want to complicate your home life. You say that Cecelia will not be jealous of me. If you say so, I will endeavor to believe it. But if I am to help you with this book, then I will regularly be in your home, and our work will punctuate our daily lives as well as Cecelia's. You must assure me that she is fine with this reality. I suppose what I am asking, Rupert, is whether or not you truly believe I will be welcome in your home to the degree that I must be there to do this work."

Rupert did not hesitate in responding. "I cannot write this book without your help, Margaret. Don't be silly. You are always welcome in my home." He paused. "My wife and I are still in the midst of unpacking today, but I look forward to seeing you and your mother at dinner. I will be very honored that the Dashwood women are our first guests."

Margaret felt at ease. This would be complicated, but she felt it would be all right in the end.

"My mother and I look forward to it," said Margaret. "Truly."

Rupert nodded to her, smiled, and then went on his way into the green countryside.

***

Margaret dressed for dinner with slightly more care than usual that night. Rupert would be sending a carriage for the Dashwood women, a luxury that Margaret had not anticipated but that she was grateful for nonetheless. She had originally thought that the cottage Rupert was leasing was the one only fifteen minutes away by foot. As it turned out, he and Cecelia had, at the last minute, opted to lease a slightly larger home — a fancier home, one that better suited a married couple. Margaret supposed it was about the same distance away, but it had enough grandeur about it that Margaret felt better about arriving in a carriage than she did on foot.

She had expected that Rupert's sabbatical year would mean that their relationship was marked by a lesser degree of formality, but now that there was the presence of Mrs. Cecelia Smith, Margaret realized that things would be much more formal than she had anticipated.

The day before, she had stood facing her mirror soaked to the bone. Now she faced the same mirror and took stock of her appearance in light of the evening before her. Margaret did not often dress for dinner. Her acquaintances in the village did not require too much adornment from her in order to feel respected, but Margaret understood that this dinner was perhaps Mrs. Smith's first evening entertaining guests in *her* home as a newly installed wife. This struck Margaret as significant, but she still could not escape the thought that Cecelia Smith barely seemed above age twenty. Margaret made a note to herself that tonight might be a good time to figure out exactly how old Cecelia was.

Margaret loved to wear black, even though she had not been in mourning since the death of her father so many years ago. But she felt that black was not an appropriate color to wear to the home of a new bride. She still wanted to make a bold choice, though. On the one hand, she wanted Cecelia to be comfortable with her. On the other hand, she was always interested in subtle messages that she might send with her appearance.

Looking in her wardrobe, the decision was suddenly easy. She would wear white. Yes, this was a sarcastic choice since now she was an old virginal spinster, but Margaret looked quite nice in white, especially white muslin adorned with lace.

After dressing herself in her long white gown and smoothing her hair, Margaret did a funny thing. She noticed a large lace doily underneath the water pitcher in her bedchamber. Without thinking, she took the doily into her hands and inspected it. She could not be sure, but she had a suspicion that this doily had been sitting on this table in this room for over a decade, and yet she had never examined it before. It was delicate, handmade, and fine. She wondered to herself if this was one of the few bits of finery that Mrs. Dashwood had stored away when they had left her late father's house. The doily was round in design and carefully knitted together like a precise and dainty spider's web.

Margaret took the doily and suddenly placed it right on top of her head. It did not *quite* look ridiculous. She only wanted to see what the effect was of wearing white with something like a veil. Margaret almost never gave a thought to wedding dresses. It did not bother her usually, but, on this particular evening as she dressed for dinner with her dearest friend and his new wife, she had a strange urge to see herself momentarily as a bride. Granted, she looked like a rather odd bride with an old doily atop her head, but her appearance in the mirror still gave the impression of youthful matrimony.

She was surprised to realize that she *liked* the way she looked dressed all in white with the silly doily atop her head. She turned her body around and watched herself in the mirror. She held her palms in front of her, clasped together as if she were holding a bouquet. She knew she was ridiculous, but she didn't care. Above all, Margaret knew the significance of gathering information — what she was doing right now was gathering information. How would a wedding dress make one feel? What does a bride feel like when she dresses for her wedding ceremony? And could she ever see herself dressed for such an occasion?

If marriage was an acceptable adventure for Rupert, maybe Margaret ought to start considering it for herself more seriously. She felt that she did not want to be left behind. As the youngest sister, this was one of her most common feelings, and there was nothing worse than the sensation of feeling left behind.

Margaret pulled the doily off of her head and then folded it neatly so that it could have its own home on her vanity table. Who knew? She might take up the doily again when the urge struck her to see herself once more as a bride. For now, though, a white dress would do.

When she came down the stairs and into the view of Mrs. Dashwood, her mother smiled at her. Mrs. Dashwood could tell that Margaret was making an effort, however slight.

"You *do* look lovely in white, my dear," said Mrs. Dashwood.

"I know, Mother," smiled Margaret. She thought privately to herself how satisfying it would be to sit in white as the only virgin at the table. She wondered if other people would notice her silent joke and find it entertaining. Rupert, at least, would notice the jest. He might laugh to himself and shake his head at Margaret — and Margaret longed for these small communications that would reveal they were still friends.

Mrs. Dashwood and Margaret rode silently

in the carriage as they made their way to Rupert and Cecelia's home. When the carriage pulled into the gravel drive, Margaret was astonished to see the size of the home. She did not often venture to this small but luxurious estate on her walks, but seeing it up close now made her realize that this was not necessarily a "modest" home for a professor. This was a gentleman's home. She wondered how Rupert could afford it on his professor's salary, but then, of course, she knew nothing of the extent of Cecelia's own fortune. Perhaps in marrying her he had come into some wealth. Inwardly, she pushed herself not to judge too hard.

Once inside, Margaret began to feel uncomfortable. She was not often ill at ease around wealth, but it felt strange to see such abundance placed in conjunction with her friend Rupert. Rupert, like Margaret, had never been wealthy. He had been comfortable but never a rich man. And he did not act as if he had the prospects of a rich man. Rupert, after all, worked for his living and taught for his supper. All of this luxury felt suddenly overwhelming to Margaret, but she resolved not to reveal her discomfort even in the slightest.

Before going into the dining room, Margaret and her mother sat with Cecelia and Rupert in the parlor drinking wine. They were waiting for Cecelia's cousin and his young daughter to arrive.

"It's quite a dreadful story," said Cecelia. "My dear cousin married long ago, but his wife died in childbirth. They had tried for many years to have a child, but, when the time finally came, her frail body could not handle it. His daughter is now nine years old. The darling's name is Marianna."

"Oh, what a lovely name," said Mrs. Dashwood. "My middle daughter's name is Marianne."

"What a sad story," said Margaret. "And in nine years' time he has never remarried?"

"No, not at all," said Cecelia. "He is devoted to little Marianna, and we cannot seem to convince him that Marianna might do well to have a woman in the home again. But, alas, he insists that he will *never* marry again. It's quite sad, but he is not at all a morose personality. He is naturally very energetic and lively. He has simply been dealt a hard hand at life, and he bears it as if it were some kind of punishment for a past wrong."

"How strange," said Margaret. "Well, I hope that we can be of cheer to him tonight."

"Oh!" exclaimed Cecelia. "There is *only* cause to be cheerful tonight! This will, in fact, be the first time that he has met my dear Rupert, and I am so happy to get to introduce him to my new friends as well!"

Margaret nodded and smiled. She was resolved to be as kind as possible to Cecelia, even though her excitement bordered on pure silliness. Cecelia looked lovely tonight, though. She was dressed in a dark rose gown that shimmered in the candlelight. Her corn colored hair looked goddess-like, twisted in a heavy knot adorned with curls at the top of her head. She looked to be a perfect picture of wifely domesticity, glowing with the thrill of matrimony. Or, at least, that's how Margaret would have described her if she had been writing a novel about this young woman. Truth be told, Margaret thought Cecelia looked very nice, but Margaret was still pleased with herself for wearing all white to dinner.

There was a flurry of sound coming from the front entrance, and it became clear that Cecelia's cousin and his little daughter had arrived for dinner. Their voices were low in the hallway, but Margaret was pleased to be able to distinguish the charming sound of the little girl's voice, who was inquiring after who they would meet that evening. Margaret loved children, and it pained her that she did not have her own little brothers or sisters to tend to.

Poor Cecelia looked like she might explode from excitement, but she endeavored to hold herself steady in the parlor to receive her cousin like a true mistress of the house. Margaret watched with amusement as Cecelia pinched her cheeks to make them glow slightly redder and tried to make her small frame a bit taller.

The doors to the parlor opened wide, and in they walked. At first, Margaret could not get a good look at them because Cecelia swarmed them like a pink blur, overwhelmed with excitement over seeing her cousins.

It was only when Margaret heard the man's

voice that she recognized him. She immediately shot a glance at her mother, who had felt the spark of recognition as well. The voice of the man before them felt like a ghost from fifteen years in the past. Neither of the Dashwood women was inclined to think of it as a friendly spirit.

After all, how could they ever be friends with Mr. John Willoughby?

Chapter Five

Though the last time Margaret had seen John Willoughby he had been in his late twenties, Margaret could still distinguish his personage even after nearly fifteen years of absence. It was him, without a doubt. His face still had the same charm, although it was now a bit more gaunt and slightly more traced with lines. His hair, which had once been rich with color, was now completely silver. Margaret suspected that this shock of silver hair made him seem even older than he actually was.

Margaret did not want to make Cecelia uncomfortable, but she was also completely unsure of how to handle this rather awkward social situation. Margaret had never told Rupert the story of Mr. Willoughby's history with the Dashwood women — she had never even mentioned his name, only a hint of his bad behavior. It was a thing of the past and she had never wanted Rupert to view her sister Marianne as lovesick.

Oh God, thought Margaret, *and this man's daughter is named Marianna.* Margaret hardly knew how to comprehend such a fact. John Willoughby probably never suspected he would encounter the Dashwood women again, but what had he been thinking to name his daughter Marianna? It was impossible to ignore the obvious association.

Several moments passed while Cecelia fawned over her cousin and did her best to introduce him to Rupert. Margaret and Mrs. Dashwood understood that they would eventually be introduced after the formal meeting between Rupert and John was finished. Cecelia was, after all, introducing her husband for the first time to an apparently beloved family member. Margaret and Mrs. Dashwood hardly knew what to say to one another. They only looked at each other with great fear. Should they be cold? Should they show kindness to John Willoughby? Friendship was impossible, of course, but they could at least be cordial for the length of an evening. Perhaps John Willoughby was not so local to the area to the extent that he would be visiting frequently. Margaret and Mrs. Dashwood knew that he was not that far away from where they lived, but he had always been just far enough to never bother them.

The family introductions now over, the inevitable moment came.

"Oh, Cousin John, I am so excited to introduce you to my new friends," said Cecelia. "Mrs. Dashwood and Miss Margaret, may I introduce to you my cousin, Mr. John Willoughby, and his beautiful daughter, Marianna Willoughby."

Marianna Willoughby, thought Margaret.

The thought did not escape her that this could have been the name of a daughter born to Mr. Willoughby and her sister Marianne. She pushed the thought aside, though, in order to confront the man before her.

His own shock was palpable, but Margaret was relieved to see that age and maturity had instilled in him a grave tactfulness.

He was the first to speak:

"Cousin Cecelia," he said, "I am, in fact, already acquainted with Mrs. Dashwood and Miss Margaret, although we have not been in one another's company for many years. Indeed, I should like to be frank with them, starting now." He faced them in earnest. "I did you great wrong fifteen years ago, and I have borne the guilt of that wrongdoing for quite some time. Although I do not deserve it, I hope you will extend me grace in the form of your acquaintance, if not in your friendship."

Margaret was rather shocked at this speech, and Mrs. Dashwood was instantly charmed. Mrs. Dashwood had always loved Willoughby and had taken great pains to make apologies for him when he had so hastily broken her daughter's heart. Margaret was less apt to forgive, but she was nonetheless impressed with his grace in this moment.

Mrs. Dashwood was the first to reply:

"Oh, Willoughby," said Mrs. Dashwood, "I only feel joy at seeing you again. The past is the past, and it will be lovely to meet you again as if for the first time."

All Margaret could say was, "It is fascinating to see you again, Willoughby." She continued, "Your fair cousin Cecelia has shown nothing but kindness to us since she arrived in the village." Margaret then leveled her eyes with John Willoughby, as if to send him a message that she would much prefer if he stayed away. "I intend to be very good friends with your cousin Cecelia." And then she smiled and ceased talking.

A small voice before them broke the tension.

"You look wonderful in white," said little Marianna, staring wide-eyed at Margaret. "You are like someone from a fairy tale."

Margaret was rather taken aback by this observation, but she had to admit to herself that it pleased her.

Margaret leaned down to little Marianna, who was a slight girl, and whispered in her ear: "That's because I am."

Marianna pulled back, her face aglow with a gasp. Willoughby smiled to see his little daughter entertained, and Margaret could tell that he was also taking stock of the Dashwood women before him. So many years had certainly changed Mrs. Dashwood and Margaret, and he was no doubt curious about the difference those years could make.

Margaret wondered what he noticed about her appearance. She favored both of her sisters, and she happened to have collected some of their best features that were also passed down from their parents. She wondered if Willoughby looked at her and saw a palimpsest of Marianne. Margaret, who always longed to be seen in light of her own individuality, hoped that he simply saw her as her own person, but the history between Willoughby and Marianne was so profound that it was highly unlikely that he did not see traces of Marianne's lips, jawline, complexion, or stature.

A perfect hostess, Cecelia exclaimed with excitement, "How wonderful that you already know each other! We will be a rather happy group tonight, then."

Margaret could tell that Cecelia was curious about what had happened between Willoughby and the Dashwood family, but her manners prevented her from prying. Margaret suspected that Cecelia would inquire privately to Margaret once their friendship was more established. Cecelia looked like the kind of young woman who couldn't resist a bit of gossip.

But what would Margaret say to her when she inevitably asked? Did she have to say anything? She thought it prudent to at least disclose to Cecelia how profoundly Willoughby had hurt Margaret's sister, but so many years had passed that it felt wrong to continue to foster animosity. Margaret was not vengeful, and she did not hold grudges well, but what Willoughby had done to Marianne was quite harsh. How could Margaret tell the story well? She was no novelist, after all.

The group finally decided to make their way into the dining room for Mrs. Cecelia Smith's debut as a dinner hostess. Margaret was surprised to see that little Marianna was allowed to sit at the table with the adults. Willoughby seemed to have anticipated the oddity of his daughter's presence and so he said unprompted, "I don't like to be away from Marianna, and we are so little around other people that I do my best to make sure she can be a part of any conversation. I assure you she is quite the conversation partner when given the chance."

"How lovely," said Mrs. Dashwood. "I do agree it is important for children to be comfortable speaking with their elders. Continual interaction with gentlemen and ladies will certainly give her an education better than any finishing school."

"I could never send her away to school even if I tried," said Willoughby.

Margaret remembered the information Cecelia had disclosed about Willoughby's past. If Marianna had entered the world as her mother left it, it made sense that Willoughby would feel strongly about keeping his young daughter as close as possible. Margaret suspected she would probably do the same thing if all she had remaining of a loved one was a miniature soul to care for.

She felt confused about the feelings she was experiencing for Willoughby at this moment. She felt a mixture of pity and fascination with his current life circumstances. He was still the same John

Willoughby, but there was something graver and more serious about him that gave Margaret pause. His newfound gravity made him seem more trustworthy and more genuine. When she had known him as a girl, he was glorious in his carelessness and his charisma. There was never a dull moment with John Willoughby. He was a man who was not afraid of exuberant feelings. He loved poetry, and his heart seemed to swell with love for Marianne. Although Margaret had only been thirteen when Willoughby entered (and exited) their lives, she trusted her memory that Willoughby loved Marianne. And when he left, she had told herself all manner of stories to excuse his behavior. It was difficult to place blame on him, and yet his rejection had nearly killed Marianne. Margaret wondered if she could ever forgive Willoughby when the memory of her sister's grave illness could not be erased from her mind.

The dinner conversation was cheerful and tame. Margaret was pleased to find herself seated next to Rupert. All day, she had been wondering about how her access to her friend would be restricted now that he was married, but their quick meeting on the hillside and now their close proximity at the dinner table gave her a bit of comfort. After the main course was being cleared, Rupert leaned over to Margaret and spoke in a low voice:

"You have never mentioned John Willoughby's name before," he said. "If the wrong that he did to your family was so profound, why did you never mention it to me?"

"Surely I've mentioned before that one of my sisters was spurned in love," Margaret whispered back.

"Is that his great wrong?'" said Rupert. "He simply spurned your sister?"

"I do not wish to speak of it right now, Rupert," Margaret hissed back. "But I will tell you that the blow was serious, and I cannot help but be uncomfortable in his presence. Now, please, drink your wine and be a good host for your wife's sake."

Rupert could sense the element of annoyance in Margaret's voice, so he moved away with his body and returned his focus to the table.

Margaret found herself rather entranced by the way Willoughby interacted with little Marianna. He involved her in the conversation, as he said he would, and openly asked her opinion about the various topics they discussed, even if she did not fully understand them. He was patient with her when she asked questions, and he delighted in her excitement over spending the evening with someone other than her dear father.

Margaret was glad that Marianne was not here to see Willoughby and his daughter at the dinner table. Marianne would not have been able to bear it. Although Marianne had a deeply happy marriage with Colonel Brandon, Margaret was always aware that the marriage had come into being simply by Colonel Brandon proving that he would never relent in caring for Marianne and protecting her. After her grave illness, brought on by the shock of Willoughby's rejection, Colonel Brandon had visited Marianne regularly, read to her, helped her get her strength back, and proved that he could be a true companion to her. There was a considerable age difference between them — more than fifteen years — but that was not so unusual.

Interestingly, there was a smaller age difference between Margaret and John Willoughby than there was between Marianne and her husband. Margaret stopped herself. Had she just made a comparison between herself and her sister? And had the counterpart of that comparison been John Willoughby himself? Margaret felt ridiculous that the thought had even crossed her mind, but now she could not escape it.

For the remainder of the evening, Margaret talked fluidly, was by all accounts jovial, and attempted to enjoy the company of her friends, but the whole time she watched Willoughby with curious discomfort. She knew that it was her duty to Rupert and the new Mrs. Smith to behave as a good guest, but, under the surface, she was rather ill at ease. Indeed, she almost felt *offended* at Willoughby's presence. It felt so strange to see Willoughby in this new environment, and she hardly knew how to categorize it in her mind. There was a degree to which his presence felt like a crude intrusion into Margaret's tranquil life, yet another shock that piled on top of her new understanding that Rupert was married and therefore entirely unavailable to Margaret's imaginative experiments in romance. In two days' time, she had experienced two great shocks. The first was Rupert's sudden marriage to Cecelia, and the other was the reappearance of John Willoughby — with a daughter whose namesake seemed to belong to his first love and not his wife. Margaret felt a bit that the gods and goddesses were all against her.

What happens to a person when forty-eight hours of one's life is consumed with shock? Margaret wondered if this is what young women on the hunt for husbands felt. It seemed to her that gentlemen were often the source of shocks, not women.

Rupert lingered with Margaret in the sitting room when the after-dinner drinks were winding down and people seemed to be ready to go home. He had looked a little uneasy all night, perhaps anxious about his new role as man of the house. Rupert did not have a particularly domineering personality, and he did not strike a person as someone who would insist upon sitting at the head of a table. He was not one to lord over other people, and Margaret could tell that he would have much preferred the original cottage he had wished to lease in the village instead of this small mansion.

"It's been a nice evening, don't you think, Margaret?" asked Rupert.

"It's been a perfectly *fine* evening," she lied, "although I've had nothing but *lovely* surprises in the past few days, and I am hopeful that tomorrow is wholly uneventful and dull."

Rupert, who usually recognized Margaret's sardonic and dry humor, took her at her word.

"Is it imprudent for me to ask for more of your history with Cousin John?" said Rupert.

"No, I don't believe it is imprudent," said Margaret. "It's only that it is a complicated story, and I was so young when it happened that I worry about my ability to tell the story well."

Rupert let his eyes rest on the little girl who looked like she was about to fall asleep at her father's side on the sofa.

"Your sister's name is Marianne, yes? Marianne Brandon?" asked Rupert. Margaret realized that he had just made the connection between her sister's name and Willoughby's daughter. Just like Margaret, Rupert did not seem to know what to make of it either.

"Time is a strange thing," he said, and then he continued to sip his brandy and stare around the room with anxiety over whether or not his guests were enjoying themselves.

The goodbyes over, Margaret and Mrs. Dashwood rode in silence once again on their way home to the cottage. What was there to say? They were too much in shock to say anything of great substance, they realized. For now, their minds warm with wine and brandy, all they could do was muse over the new information they had learned and the reemergence of an old acquaintance they had both resolved to forget entirely.

***

The next morning, Mrs. Dashwood and Margaret sat stoically over their tea and muffins.

"Do you think we ought to tell Marianne?" asked Mrs. Dashwood.

"Of course, mother," said Margaret. "We will have to tell her eventually. We cannot pretend that we are not now reacquainted with John Willoughby. He is a part of our lives now, at least for the year of Rupert's sabbatical."

"I suppose there is no way to avoid him," said Mrs. Dashwood.

"No, there is not," said Margaret. "I will not let Mr. Willoughby stand in the way of my friendship with Rupert and my intention to help him with his book during his sabbatical. Willoughby took away my sister's happiness all those years ago. I will not let him take away my one year of being close to my best friend."

"I suppose you're right," said Mrs. Dashwood. "We will have to endure the acquaintance as best as we can manage, although I don't see how it would be all that difficult. Willoughby is a lovely person, despite how he wronged Marianne. Even now after all these years, I cannot fully blame Willoughby for his behavior. In many ways, you can't blame anyone for being worried about money. That is something that I understand immensely."

"It is clear that we will be seeing him often," said Margaret. "It strikes me that Mrs. Smith does not have a great many family members, at least not those that are close by. Mr. Willoughby may be more like a brother to her than a cousin. Yes, I believe we will see him and little Marianna quite a bit."

"Oh," moaned Mrs. Dashwood, "I had almost forgotten about the child. What do you think persuaded him to name the child Marianna? It's almost like something out of a novel."

"Well, it *is* Willoughby, mother," said Margaret. "He had a tendency to live his life as if he were the hero of a novel, which accounts for a great deal of his self-centeredness."

"But, Margaret, did you not find him quite repentant last night, especially in his first words to us?"

"Of course I found him repentant," said Margaret, "but if there is anything I remember about Willoughby, it's that he was inherently eloquent. I hope that his words were genuine, but, after his behavior toward Marianne, I don't know how trustworthy his words are,"

"My darling," said Mrs. Dashwood, "you were only a child when Willoughby left us."

"That does not mean I have forgotten all of the pain he caused," said Margaret indignantly. "And it was almost more awful for me because I was so young and no one would tell me the full extent of what was happening. This is what I remember about that time of our lives: I remember that Edward was here, and then he was gone. I remember that Willoughby was here, and then he was gone. I remember that Colonel Brandon was here, and *he* never left, and I remember that Edward returned only when his horrible mother could not control him any longer."

"Mother," Margaret continued, "what I remember of that time was that all of the gentlemen who surrounded us came and went as they pleased. We were at their mercy when it came to the gift of their presence. Our lives were punctuated by *waiting*, and I believe that Willoughby was the worst perpetrator of this horrible pattern in which we found ourselves. So, I hope you will forgive me if I question his repentance."

Mrs. Dashwood raised her eyebrows and returned to her tea. Margaret abandoned her posture and leaned back in her chair. She let her head tilt back so that she could inspect the ceiling and all of its little imperfections. The dents and scratches and occasional water stains seemed to create a bland and dreary map of Margaret's little world. Margaret had always wished that her world was more expansive, but the thought of Willoughby made her realize that her domain was permeable to intruders. Instead of her world being filled with fascinating new people from all over the globe, she was forced to deal with returning pilgrims who had only done wrong during their initial visit.

And propriety required that she bid them warm welcome.

Chapter Six

Margaret's first morning of work with Rupert began smoothly enough with strong tea and good morning light in the study, but Margaret was constantly distracted by her own self-consciousness. She worried about things as small as whether or not she was sitting too close to Rupert in the library. They were both sharing the same concordance of Shakespeare's works, so they had to be in some proximity to one another. Cecelia was also in the library with them. Cecelia tried very hard to assume a posture of studiousness during their time together, but it became clear very quickly that she was unsure how to be helpful. At first, Cecelia made it a point to keep them in constant supply of tea and scones. This was fine for the first forty-five minutes of the work session, but after that she became unsure of how to further help.

Margaret sensed her listlessness and tried to intervene. Even though the circumstances were not what she expected, Margaret nonetheless wanted to be a good friend to Cecelia. She considered that this might be her first official act of friendship.

"Mrs. Smith," said Margaret, "I wonder if you might help me with a bit of research I am doing at present?"

"Oh, please call me Cecelia!" said Cecelia. Margaret was relieved at this gesture. She had gone back and forth in her head about what would be acceptable to call her, especially since Margaret and Rupert were so close. Calling each other by their Christian names perfectly suited Margaret.

"And I do hope you will call me Margaret," she said in reply. "Now, what I need from you is to have you begin the process of reading through *Henry IV* Part 1 line by line so that you can be on the lookout for specific language that describes *any* of the female characters in this play. You see, your dear husband is rather convinced that his book on the history plays need not focus too intently on the presence of women. I, however, disagree — and part of my contribution is to give him everything he needs in order to add women to the story."

"So you wish me to read and take notes whenever a woman is described?" asked Cecelia.

"Exactly. That would be most helpful. I am working through my own notes on the other plays," said Margaret, "but *Henry IV* Part 1 is a text that I have not had time to get to just yet. Do you think you can manage it?"

"Oh, of course!" squealed Cecelia. "I am just ever so glad to be helpful, you know."

"I do, my dear," replied Margaret. "Now, let's get to work."

For a few moments it seemed that this assignment for Cecelia would bring them to a state of harmony. As the three of them worked together, they sunk into a profound working silence — the only sounds in the room coming from their pen scratches and rustling papers. For several minutes, Margaret felt a state of bliss. Yes, she could do this every morning if this was what it would be like.

But the silence didn't last very long. Cecelia became restless, and she had hardly passed through the first few scenes of the play. She would intermittently release heavy sighs and then glance up at her coworkers to see if they noticed. Out of the corner of her eye, Margaret watched Cecelia squint at the pages as if she were reading and rereading what was before her. Margaret wondered how frequently Cecelia read Shakespeare. As the daughter of a professor, Cecelia likely had read many of the more popular works, but there was no telling whether or not she had actually enjoyed reading them. Margaret often assumed that people enjoyed Shakespeare, but that assumption had gotten her into many awkward conversations with people who did not share her enthusiasm for the Bard.

Margaret decided she would wait just a moment before asking if Cecelia was quite well. Cecelia began to slump in the chair she was sitting in, her whole body collapsing toward the pages in front of her. She looked uneasy, uncomfortable, and bored. It had hardly been fifteen minutes.

"Cecelia," asked Margaret, "are you feeling alright?"

"Oh, yes!" Cecelia perked up. "I am fine. Rupert knows that I am not a great reader, and so I find myself growing tired after only a few pages!"

Margaret wasn't sure how to respond to this. She had tried to give Cecelia a task to do, but it seemed that this task would be insufficient for Cecelia's entertainment. Margaret, for her part, was frustrated that she must take into account Cecelia's attention in addition to the needs of the book.

Rupert added his own comment:

"My dear," he said, "you are by no means bound to help with this work. I know that it is quite dull to be cooped up in a library all morning. If you don't wish to stay, I will not make you. Remember, too, darling, that it was you who expressed interest in assisting with the work. Perhaps it would be enough if I simply shared with you my progress over tea later."

Cecelia looked a little hurt, but her beautiful face hid much of this emotion from Rupert. Margaret understood that Cecelia deeply desired to be helpful to her new husband, but the fact of the matter was that his work was deeply uninteresting to her. Margaret had no idea how to remedy this fact; all she could do was sit as a silent observer while Cecelia and Rupert stared at each other. Rupert did not want to hurt Cecelia's feelings, but it seemed that he was doing just that.

"I think perhaps I will try a little longer," said Cecelia. "I don't find this play particularly compelling, but there is no harm in reading a bit more, even if it is only for my own edification!"

A diplomatic response, thought Margaret. They all returned to their work

On a piece of paper in front of her, Margaret was mapping out a list of claims that she hoped to bring forward to Rupert by the end of the morning. She was rather taken with the character of Lady Percy, Hotspur's wife from *Henry IV* Part 1, the play she had given to Cecelia to read. (Offering this text to Cecelia had been admittedly a bit of a ruse. Margaret knew the play intimately, and she did not necessarily need Cecelia to take notes on it, but she wanted to give her something to do.)

What Margaret liked about Lady Percy was that she was willing to argue vehemently with her husband. Even though she only appeared in two scenes in the play, she made her presence known by arguing distinctly with Hotspur. Margaret wished that Shakespeare had spent more time writing about this odd relationship, one that showed how fiery a woman could be when she was trying to talk sense into her beloved.

Margaret had never really experienced that sensation of needing to talk sense to someone she loved, at least not someone she loved romantically

(which was no one). She often found herself arguing with her mother, but those arguments always
occurred in good humor. *What would it be like*, she
thought, *to be filled with a passion over something
so strong that she screamed at a lover so they would
understand? Where did such a swell of feeling come
from? What made someone scream with passion?*

And she really did mean "scream," not "yell."
There's something about the word *scream* that indicated a total release and abandonment of propriety. Women often only screamed when they were
in danger or frightened — what would it be like if
they screamed about justice or truth? What would
it be like if they screamed aloud their thoughts and
desires to someone who was not listening? This
was a strange tangent for Margaret to be on while
she puttered with her notes, but she just couldn't
escape the thought.

Would she ever feel compelled to scream
at Rupert? She wasn't sure. She felt confident,
though, that Rupert would eventually find a
reason to scream at her, although such an event
had not come to pass as of yet (thank goodness).

Margaret looked over at Cecelia, who was
waning once more. She tried to glance and see how
far Cecelia had gotten in the text. She was still very
much in Act One.

Margaret sighed. Perhaps, in time, Cecelia
would warm up to the nature of the work, or perhaps she never would.

Cecelia slowly and quietly closed her book.

Margaret noticed that she did not even place a scrap of paper in between the pages in order to hold her place.

Cecelia stood and spoke:

"I think I require a walk around the garden," she said plaintively. "I suspect the two of you will be just fine without me, but I anticipate a full report of your progress at tea time," she smiled.

"My darling, are you sure?" asked Rupert. "Perhaps there is another task that we can find for you to do other than reading?"

"Oh, Rupert," replied Cecelia, "your work concerns books — there is no way to do work that concerns books without *reading*, of that I am sure."

She smiled at the two of them, placed the book back on the table, and left. Although the absence of her physical beauty made the library feel a bit more dull than it had been before, Margaret felt that the atmosphere of the room became lighter and more airy. No longer tasked with entertaining Cecelia, Margaret and Rupert could simply work — and work they did. They barely whispered a word to each other over the course of the next few hours before luncheon. But even in their silence, they worked together convivially. Whenever Margaret felt that she had made a profound discovery, her face would light up, and Rupert would not be able to help noticing her elation. He would smile at the recognition of her discovery, perhaps chuckle a little, and then they would return to work.

Margaret liked sitting in silence with Rupert. They always had plenty to talk about, but there was something about the silence that was restful and comforting. To be silent in someone's presence for hours at a time is to learn keenly how their presence alters a room. Words in conversation can sometimes muddy the sense of presence, but silence and stillness can communicate multitudes. Margaret and Rupert were not bothersome to one another; they had no offending habits that annoyed the other person. They knew how to simply *be* with one another. Margaret felt that this was a true gift, something not to be disregarded.

The silence also gave Margaret some time to reflect on her own expectations for something like marriage. Seeing her dearest friend married made it so that she couldn't help thinking about whether or not marriage was something *she* needed to consider. If she could find someone to sit in silence with, then perhaps marriage would not be so odd after all. Yes, she felt that silence would be the true test of whether or not matrimony suited her. It was very hard to perform such a test, though. The only reason Rupert and Margaret were able to be alone together was because of their long friendship, one that had long since given up the need for a chaperone.

Margaret still wondered if Cecelia was uneasy leaving the two of them in the library together. If anything, Cecelia was probably just sad that it was too troublesome for her to be included in the work. Margaret and Rupert would never say such a thing explicitly, but it seemed very likely that they both felt it.

Margaret looked out the window of the library that overlooked the garden in front of the estate. She saw Cecelia in a beautiful red gown and black cape walking the grounds and inspecting the various flowers that would soon be killed by the first frost. Based on the way her body moved in the garden, Margaret tried to perceive if Cecelia was hurt. If she was, her body did not show it — at least not overtly. She walked regally in the garden with the posture of the lady of the house.

What would Margaret look and act like if she were the lady of her own house? Margaret knew herself well, and so she suspected that she would spend most of her time in the library of her imaginary great estate. Indeed, Margaret felt that she would be a rather terrible lady of the house. But before she could think about it any further, she noticed that Cecelia was no longer alone. A gentleman had joined her in the garden, and it did not take long for Margaret to perceive who it was.

It was John Willoughby, of course, visiting his dear cousin on a beautiful fall morning.

***

Willoughby joined them for luncheon that afternoon. Little Marianna was not with him, which surprised Margaret, but Willoughby explained that in the mornings she was attended to by a tutor. Willoughby had tried to be her tutor himself but found that, though his little daughter loved him dearly, even she grew tired of Papa. So he left her with a tutor and music teacher who gave her exactly the kind of education that a young man would receive. Willoughby took pride in this. He believed heartily that women ought to be educated in just the same way as men. As he explained this while they dined, Margaret felt her insides surge with a sense of affirmation of his ideas. She, too, believed that women ought to be educated in the same way as men, and it frustrated her that there was not an avenue for her to attend university.

"I am very glad to hear it, Mr. Willoughby," said Margaret. "Perhaps by the time Marianna is of age, they will finally admit young women into the universities. We women cannot be denied entry to the guild of scholars for much longer. I guarantee you, the time will come when we will rebel."

"I don't doubt it," said Willoughby. "I am intent on giving Marianna the best education possible. My deepest desire is that knowledge will help her attain a degree of self-awareness. I don't mean to speak poorly of women, of course, but it has been my experience that young women often lack an ability to put words to their feelings and to be reflective about what they're actually experiencing."

Margaret nearly choked on her salad. "Mr. Willoughby, what can you mean?" she said.

"Again, I do not mean to be rude," said Willoughby, "but I have often found that women, particularly young ladies, don't tell me what their true feelings are. I can only assume that they don't tell me because they are not aware themselves of what those feelings are."

"You are quite mistaken, Mr. Willoughby," said Margaret. "I have a sense that women know quite well what their feelings are, but we exist in a society that demands women keep quiet, be demure, and always play the passive role in their relationships. A woman has rarely told you what she really feels, I fear, because she herself understands the profound social consequences that accompany such an action. If we state the full range of our feelings, we risk being called hysterical or irrational. We also risk being perceived as too bold or overly masculine — ridiculous perceptions, in my opinion. Everything is stacked against us if we speak our true thoughts and practice honesty. I say this to you plainly, Mr. Willoughby, because I think it is quite important that you, as the father to a daughter, ought to know the social rules that your lovely little daughter will undoubtedly encounter."

Willoughby looked a bit shocked at Margaret's response. It was clear that he was not used to having young women speak to him so directly. Margaret wondered if her sister Marianne had ever spoken to him so directly before. She suspected, though, that everything Marianne had said to Willoughby was drenched in poetry to begin with; if he had not perceived Marianne's true feelings, then it may have been simply because he was not sensitive to poetic flair.

But as Margaret spoke sense to him at the table, she faintly recalled her fleeting thought earlier that morning of what it would be like to scream at someone she loved. She did not love Mr. Willoughby, and she did not wish to scream at him, but she suspected that this sort of indignation was akin to the thought experiment she had performed earlier.

"But if women do not begin to speak plainly," said Willoughby, "then this societal wrong, as you imply it is, will likely never dissipate. Why do more women not speak up about this reality?"

"Oh, Cousin John," cut in Cecelia, "I must agree with Miss Margaret. It never did me any favors when I spoke honestly about my feelings. I like to think of myself as an easygoing young woman, but even Papa becomes uncomfortable when I tell him too much of what is in my mind."

Willoughby was further surprised to hear his cousin Cecelia agree with Margaret. Only Rupert sat in silence, not particularly interested in any sort of confrontation. Margaret wondered why he seemed reluctant to speak up against Willoughby — why did Rupert appear so resigned?

Willoughby spoke again. "I suppose this is a subject that I am not as well-versed in as I first suspected. My apologies, ladies."

"Apology accepted," Margaret said, smiling. "Now, would the two of you like to hear about the work that Rupert and I did this morning?"

Successfully changing the subject, Margaret

and Rupert talked of how they had spent their time together plotting out a core purpose for the book — what would its thesis be, what sort of argument would it attempt to advance, and etc. Margaret and Rupert were lively in their recounting of the morning's work, but Cecelia bore the account rather quietly. It was clear that this was not interesting to her, but Rupert especially was resolved to make sure Cecelia was at least familiar with his work (Willoughby, for his part, actually seemed rather intrigued).

Cecelia listened diligently, and she tried to affect a posture of keen interest. She asked simple questions about the plays and the characters, and she did her best to share in Rupert's enthusiasm whenever he seemed excited about a particular topic. Surely Rupert and Cecelia had spoken of his work before, but this was perhaps the first time that Cecelia had ever been on display (it was only luncheon, but it must have felt like a stage to Cecelia) while learning about his endeavors as a scholar. Margaret watched with interest as Cecelia did her best to lean into the role of professor's wife. Cecelia probably would do much better with the more social aspects of being a faculty wife, but, for now, she did well over luncheon.

Margaret, for her part, was simply satisfied with the good morning of work. She had been so worried about what things would look like, but today's experience made her feel that Rupert's sabbatical year would be a fruitful one — not just for him, but for herself as well. Luncheon over, Margaret announced her thanks for a wonderful morning and meal. She told Rupert that she intended to return at the same time tomorrow, and then she rose from the table in order to begin her long walk back home.

Mr. Willoughby surprised her, though, by asking, "Miss Margaret, would you object to me escorting you back to the cottage? I would very much like to accompany you."

"Yes, that's fine," said Margaret. "I always love company on a long walk."

"Excellent," said Willoughby.

Margaret looked at him quizzically. She had expected that Mr. Willoughby would want to do the noble thing and reestablish some friendly terms with the Dashwood women, at least for the sake of propriety, but she did not expect him to make a move so quickly. She suspected that most moments Willoughby spent around a Dashwood woman only brought him pain over his past mistakes, which perhaps made him reluctant. But he seemed oddly excited at the prospect of walking alongside Margaret through the moors.

What will we talk about, though? thought Margaret. The only thing they truly had in common was his history with Marianne. That was it. Margaret remembered that he had had a great love of literature when he was courting her sister, but Margaret was not sure that he would wish to discuss books when the personal history they shared seemed all the more significant. As much as we may resist it, life is nearly always more interesting than books. That books are more entrancing is perhaps a myth we tell ourselves when we are not sufficiently interested in parsing out the wonder and excitement of our own lives.

Their cloaks and hats secured, Margaret Dashwood and John Willoughby made their way out into the cool afternoon.

***

They were awkward at first, commenting upon the weather and inquiring about health. It was a glorious day, and Margaret was glad to be out of the stuffy library and in the autumn sunshine. The leaves on the trees were only just now beginning to turn, and it made her feel great pleasure to see little splatters of yellow and orange in the trees that were scattered among the moors. She loved autumn. She always found it to be a profound relief after the heat of summer. Autumn also brought a reprieve from social engagements — when the air turned cooler, there were fewer group outings and picnics. She was glad to have the quiet that accompanied the fall season, but the presence of John Willoughby beside her made her wonder if this year's autumn would not be as peaceful as in years past.

Margaret could feel herself becoming winded. John Willoughby was significantly taller than she, and so she had to quicken her pace in order to keep up with him. When there came a point where his speed conflicted with her enjoyment of the walk, she finally spoke.

"Mr. Willoughby, I beg you to consider that my legs are significantly shorter than yours," she said. "Would you do me the kindness of slowing down, please?"

He laughed. "I'm sorry, Miss Margaret," he said with a smile. "I'm afraid my pace always increases when I am nervous."

"Nervous?" said Margaret. "Why are you nervous?"

"Because," he said, "I am walking in the countryside with a young woman who has only the *worst* opinion of me, and there is likely nothing I can do to revise that opinion — other than to put on a good face for the *next* fifteen years. Perhaps only then she and her mother will see fit to forgive me."

"Mr. Willoughby," said Margaret, "you have our forgiveness." She paused and then continued, "But I'm sure you understand that forgiveness does not mean trust."

"Oh, undoubtedly," he said, "you should not trust me, but I am grateful that you forgive me."

Margaret was surprised that his comment made her laugh. In fact, it was a comment that bore the basic traits of comedy. Comedy, Margaret believed, must surprise the recipient with its truthfulness. And there was great truthfulness in what Willoughby had said.

"You laugh at me," said Willoughby with a

smirk.

"How can I not?" said Margaret. "You believe yourself to be a true rogue, and I must admit that I believe the same."

"I used to be a rogue," said Willoughby, "but now I am only paying the price for a youth spent in constant roguishness."

"It's been fifteen years," said Margaret. "Surely you have been able to escape your reputation with new friends and acquaintances. You only bring up your roguishness because I saw firsthand how brutal you could be."

"I was brutal, wasn't I?" said Willoughby. He was serious now. Margaret worried that she had gone too far in their convivial conversation. She had thought him quite amiable, but now she worried but he was in fact sensitive about his past wrongs. Margaret never liked to upset anyone, but it was strange to think that she might have the power to offend one of her sister's lost loves.

Margaret decided that all she could do was match him in his new seriousness.

"You were not necessarily brutal by intent," said Margaret, "but you were careless, and carelessness has an inescapable brutality to it when cast upon a young woman. Wouldn't you agree, Mr. Willoughby?"

"I was careless," he said, "but I hope you will understand that I was also desperate. I had a whole plan before me that would have allowed me to marry your sister, but my one benefactor had other plans. I was young, I had no profession other than my name, and I saw no prospects before me. If I had married your sister, we would have been quite destitute."

"Do you really think Marianne would have minded it?" asked Margaret, now becoming a little indignant.

"In time, I think she would have," said Willoughby. "I am not saying anything against your sister's character. We loved each other with youthful enthusiasm, but you must understand that, if I had chosen to marry her, I would have had nothing to give her. Absolutely nothing. The only thing I could do to maintain my pride was to leave as quickly as possible. I thought perhaps that my leaving would also serve her sense of pride. I did not want to prolong any pain. It was mere chance that we saw one another in London that time. Seeing her again was not my wish, even though I thought of her constantly."

Margaret was struck by how plainly he spoke of his carelessness with Marianne. He also spoke of it in terms of money, something that did not surprise her. But she was shocked by how little he held back. Of course, he must have understood that when everything was happening so many years ago, Margaret had been still a child. She supposed that thirteen stood somewhere between childhood and young womanhood, but she thought that Willoughby had viewed her as a little girl.

"Mr. Willoughby," said Margaret, "I wonder if you have forgotten that I was there, too. I saw your romance with Marianne happen right before my eyes. You were by her side every day. As each week passed, I grew excited to see which grand gesture you would throw at her next. Marianne believed that you were the most wonderful man she had ever encountered. You had such charm and joy that followed you everywhere — you made our lives so exciting. How can you then speak so flippantly — and, dare I say, economically — about your relations with our family?"

"Surely the excitement of the Dashwood family did not rely upon me alone," said Willoughby. He was not angry with her. Instead, he was quite interested in what she had to say. He showed his interest in her statements by slowing down his pace and turning his body toward her, even though she resolutely kept her face forward.

"Oh, Mr. Willoughby," exclaimed Margaret, "don't you understand a family of women, such as we Dashwood women are, have lives that are punctuated by the excitement of gentlemen coming and going into our sphere of being? I'm not saying that I approve of our way of life. I merely state its antecedents. We are always waiting, it seems. I remember waiting for you to make up your mind — indeed, I was quite sure that you and Marianne were engaged. Marianne, of course, told us nothing, but when you left I realized that all of our waiting had been in vain. I don't believe you had any profound consideration for our feelings. If you had, I think you would have given us a more robust reason for your departure."

"Miss Margaret," he said, "you assume that I did have a robust reason. I was only looking out for myself — *that* I hope you will understand."

"But how could you have been so cruel?" she said finally.

"Because I was young and knew nothing of how easy it was to bring pain to someone whom one loved," he said. "Now I understand that phenomenon immensely."

"Do you?" said Margaret.

"I do," he said. "You want something from me, do you not? You want some kind of apology that goes beyond what I stated to you and your mother last night. I don't blame you for it, but I wish you would tell me what other information you desire to know. If you name it, I will tell it to you. I have no desire to withhold information from you, especially if it will help you see that I mean no ill will toward your family."

Margaret thought about what Willoughby said for a long moment. He was right: He had apologized and she and her mother had accepted the apology, in word if not in spirit. What was it that she wanted from him? Was there anything he could possibly say that would ever bring her peace about what he had done to Marianne? Breaking someone's heart is not an unforgivable offence; it is only marked with deep sadness, and it had been so many years since the shock of that heartbreak had taken place. Had Marianne's wounds healed? Had *Margaret's* healed? Although she had not experienced the betrayal on the same level as her sister, she had still felt abandoned when Willoughby left. In Willoughby, she had thought she was going to gain an exuberant older brother. He had teased her with the hope of their family's expansion, and then he had left. It wasn't that Margaret was dissatisfied with her brothers-in-law, Colonel Brandon and Edward Ferrars; it was just that Willoughby had done something rather particular to her heart.

Margaret understood, of course, that what she had experienced was a youthful crush, perhaps her first ever crush and her first swell of young love. It was forbidden, obviously, since the subject of her love was connected to her sister, but she had still felt quite strongly for Willoughby. Even though she had only been thirteen, her heart had swelled for him, which made it all the more painful when he had left. Margaret considered that this was a rather interesting situation for a young woman to find herself in: She was re-encountering a man whom she had felt youthful attraction for when she was a mere thirteen-year-old girl. Now, as a twenty-eight-year-old woman, she was encountering that man again, and with that encounter came all of the old feelings and all of the old confusions. What *did* she want from him? What did she need in order to move on?

After a moment, she realized what she wanted to ask.

"I have offered you forgiveness," said Margaret, "and I give it truthfully, but I still have so many questions. I wonder if you might *advise* me, Mr. Willoughby. Many years ago, I thought that you would be an older brother to me, and then I felt as though that privilege was torn away. In an older brother, I hoped for someone who could give me advice. I am lucky, granted, to have Mr. Ferrars and Colonel Brandon in my life, but you know as well as I do that they're quite different from you. I want to know *your* opinion of some things. If I asked you candidly, would you tell me the truth?"

"It depends upon the question, I suppose," said Willoughby.

"No, that answer is not sufficient for me. I wish for you to be open to any question I ask you," proclaimed Margaret.

He seemed a little surprised by her forwardness, but he nodded and said, "I will do my best to, Miss Margaret."

"Very well then," said Margaret. "I have some questions about love."

Chapter Seven

Margaret actually had quite a few questions about love. The past few days had aroused several new musings in her mind. What did love *feel* like? What was love capable of? How did you know if you were in love? Could you *choose* to be in love with someone? What does love do to one's body? How does love change once a person is married? Her questions were endless, but they were not unreasonable. They were questions that came from a young woman who had little experience other than novels and who earnestly wished to take a scientific approach to the conceptual nature of romance.

The first question she posed to Willoughby on that walk was: "Mr. Willoughby, how do you know that you are in love?"

"Miss Margaret," he said, "I don't even know where to begin. Love is not necessarily something that comes with verifiable proof. It is an action, I believe, but it is not something you can codify."

"Oh, I highly doubt that," said Margaret. "I'm of the opinion that everything can be codified, so long as you know how to pay close enough attention."

"Very well then," said a resigned Willoughby. "Love is all-consuming, as you have probably guessed from your books. It makes it impossible to work and very challenging to think clearly. For instance, I was obviously in love with your sister because it resulted in me making horrible decisions at the end. I had no foresight because I was absorbed in feelings of love. My love for your sister, I suppose I am saying, is part of what made me leave."

"Well, that's rather discouraging," said Margaret.

"I know," added Willoughby. "I would also say that the depth of love does not necessarily align with what one can do practically. One's real life always invades the veneer of love. An accomplished romantic, in my opinion, is someone who can hold both of those worlds in tension — the world of love and the world of one's actual life."

"And have you ever been successful with such a balance, Mr. Willoughby?" asked Margaret.

"Only with Marianne — I'm sorry, I mean Marianna," he said.

Margaret felt a little uneasy. She did not wish to discuss the comparison between her sister and his daughter, but his verbal mishap had revealed that he too struggled with their separation.

Margaret decided to ignore the mistake.

"You mean to say that your love for your

daughter and your commitment to being practical about your family's life are not in conflict with one another?" asked Margaret.

"Yes," he said, "and I believe that this is the truest and most honorable vision of love that I have experienced in my life."

"I don't doubt it," said Margaret. "Marianna is a fine young girl. I'm sure she will grow up feeling quite loved and cared for, even with only one parent."

"Miss Margaret," he said, "is there any particular reason why you are so curious about love? Are you yourself in love?"

"No!" said Margaret. "I am absolutely not in love — or, at least, not to my knowledge. Indeed, I don't believe there is anyone in my immediate vicinity with whom I could be in love, a rather frustrating prospect, I suppose, if one has any interest at all in romance." This comment was not entirely true, but she said it nonetheless.

"If you truly do have some interest in romance," said Willoughby, "you will want to talk with my cousin Cecelia. She has much more experience with matters of love than I do."

"Cecelia?" said Margaret. "I'm not sure I feel confident asking advice from such a young woman."

"Well, she has found herself married," replied Willoughby. "That has to count for something."

"I suppose," said Margaret. "Mr. Willoughby,

how old is your cousin Cecelia?"

"I believe she turned twenty right before her marriage to Rupert," said Willoughby.

"Twenty!" Margaret exclaimed. "I confess, this is the age I thought she was, but it is hard to hear it confirmed. I am eight years older than her — I don't know that I could be prevailed upon to trust the advice of someone so much younger."

"Well," said Willoughby, "just because she's young does not mean she is inexperienced. The past five years or so have introduced her to a great deal of romance — and heartbreak. Again, I must confess that I was quite surprised when I received word of her quick engagement to your friend Rupert. It was not what I expected."

Margaret looked at him pointedly. "Do you mean to say that Rupert was not what you expected?" Margaret had little patience for any comment that approached an insult of her dearest friend.

"No, no," said Willoughby, "Rupert is quite a gentleman, and I am glad to have him in the family. But Cecelia had been connected to another young man before Rupert, and when I received her letter, I expected that she would be announcing her engagement to this other gentleman, not your friend."

"Another gentleman?" said Margaret. "How surprising! Is it imprudent for me to ask for more details, Mr. Willoughby?"

"Yes," said Willoughby, "but I suspect you

will ask me anyway. You are a Dashwood, after all."

Margaret laughed. He was right — this was one area in which she was quite similar to her sister Marianne. Marianne liked to know everything, sometimes to her own detriment. Mrs. Dashwood also had the same enthusiasm for a bit of gossip, and Margaret herself was not immune to this interest. Margaret exercised a degree of propriety in her response to Mr. Willoughby, if only to improve his impression of her.

"You may tell me whatever you believe is useful," said Margaret. "I have asked you about romance — if there is something to be learned from your cousin's past, and you feel comfortable sharing it, then I am resolved to be a student of it."

"The only reason I feel comfortable sharing it with you," said Willoughby, "is because I know my cousin Cecelia, and I know without a doubt that she will tell you everything anyway. You must promise me that when she does tell you all, you will pretend to be surprised."

Margaret smiled. "You have my word."

Willoughby then began to share about the tumultuous four years that had preceded Cecelia's first encounter with Rupert. Cecelia had come out in London at age sixteen, beautiful and sought after by plenty of gentlemen. Cecelia was the youngest child, and so her parents had a tendency to fawn over her, particularly when it came to her prospects for marriage.

Cecelia had found herself holding the attention of a gentleman who was younger than her normal suitors. Walter Brooke was a young man with a great deal of money, but he was only twenty-one years old. Even though he was wealthy, his family did not feel that he was in an appropriate position to marry. But Walter had been enamored with Cecelia and Cecelia was enchanted by him, as well. Willoughby explained how the two young people had maintained a secret engagement for nearly three years, unbeknownst to anyone. They exchanged letters under pseudonyms and made plans without any of their family members realizing what they were up to.

Trouble arose, however, when Walter's parents attempted to push Walter into a marriage with another wealthy young woman whose family would help form a fine alliance with the Brooke family. Poor Cecelia, who was a lovely young woman of means but was nonetheless a professor's daughter, was not deemed to be a reasonable match for Walter. What Walter did not tell Cecelia was that he kept up the ruse of being amenable to his parents' wishes, all the way up until his parents asked Walter to not only propose, but also to agree to a wedding date.

Walter, who was overwhelmed with frustration over his situation, finally plotted with Cecelia for the two of them to run away and elope. They made it as far as a respectable inn just outside of London, but Walter was recognized by another young man dining at the inn. Walter was flustered in the presence of this other gentleman, and he could not bring himself to a place of bravery in announcing his intentions with Cecelia.

Apparently, when Cecelia found herself confronted with Walter's lack of courage, she promptly requested that he return her to her father's home with all speed.

When Willoughby was finished, Margaret said, "It seems that your cousin Cecelia is wiser than I give her credit for."

"She is no fool," said Willoughby, "but it is not difficult for her to be swept up in the flurry of romance. You see, when I received word of her engagement, I had expected that she and Mr. Brooke had come to some sort of agreement — perhaps they had forgiven one another and they would be married after all. But instead I saw your friend Rupert's name in the letter.

"How much time had passed between the broken secret engagement with Mr. Brooke and Cecelia's engagement to Rupert?" asked Margaret.

"Now that is a prime question," said Willoughby. "I am not sure. I only know it was fast. But I do not blame her — you see, I also have a history of moving on quite hastily."

"There you are wrong," said Margaret. "You had a great deal of choice in the matter. Women like myself and Cecelia have autonomy only insofar as gentlemen permit it. This you know is true, Mr. Willoughby."

Willoughby sighed. "I will not argue with

you."

"No," said Margaret, "there is absolutely no use in arguing with me. I must say, though, I'm rather relieved to hear that your cousin Cecelia has not had it entirely easy. She is so lively and beautiful that I expected that her experience of love and marriage was rather idyllic. But I can see now that I was wrong. I believe I now respect her a bit more, actually. I often find myself enlarging my respect for other women who have struggled in one way or another."

"I feel the same," said Willoughby. "Suffering enhances character tremendously." He paused and then continued. "Have you met with great suffering, Miss Margaret?"

"Not necessarily in love," said Margaret, "but I have suffered through others' opinions of my singleness. I came out in London ten years ago and have not found myself married in all of that time. I confess I am not wildly interested in matrimony, but I am starting to consider it now. Rupert is my dearest friend, and if he feels that matrimony is something of value, then I have a desire to respect that opinion."

"You speak of it all quite methodically," said Willoughby. "You understand, of course, that marriage is so much more than a social arrangement, don't you?"

"Of course I understand that," said Margaret, "but I am nonetheless curious about whether or not this social arrangement is something to which

I could be amenable."

"So then," said Willoughby, "you are thinking of getting married? May I ask who the lucky gentleman is?"

"This is my problem," said Margaret, "I am thinking of marriage very tentatively and cautiously — but I, as of yet, have no gentleman in mind."

"Well, I wish him luck, whoever he is," said Willoughby.

They had reached the path that led to Margaret and Mrs. Dashwood's cottage. Margaret turned to Willoughby and was rather struck by how strange it felt to see him so much older with the landscape of her home in the background. In a way, it was like being visited by a ghost, and she felt a shiver slink down to the bottom of her spine.

Suddenly, she saw herself as a thirteen-year-old girl again, helplessly watching her sister fall in love with Mr. Willoughby. She remembered their picnics on the lawn in the spring months — a much younger Margaret had collected posies and made daisy chains while she attempted to insert herself into Willoughby and Marianne's high-minded conversations. In her memory, there was a kind of halo of light around Willoughby and her sister. Margaret had never forgotten how beautiful they looked together. As a thirteen-year-old, Margaret had badly wanted to grow up in such a way that she might become her own version of Marianne. Marianne had been all joy and light, especially when Willoughby had been in their lives. Some of that light still remained in her older sister, but her long illness after Willoughby's betrayal had made Margaret realize just how easily a light might be dimmed.

She decided she might like to state this plainly to Willoughby, who was waiting to say goodbye.

"My sister was never quite the same after you left," said Margaret gravely. "I am sure you suspected this, but I wish to confirm it for you now. If I have long been suspicious of romance, it is because only now am I brave enough to risk what my sister endured." Margaret paused. "I believe you already know that the grief nearly killed her."

Willoughby looked at the ground. He seemed to understand that Margaret did not require a verbal response; she only wished him to hear her words.

After a moment, he raised his eyes and held out his hands. "May we shake hands, Miss Margaret?" he asked. "And if you will submit to being my friend, I hope you and your mother will join me for a picnic at my estate in two days' time. I would very much like for all of us to become more reacquainted with one another, Rupert and Cecelia included."

Margaret shook his hand firmly. "We would not miss it, Mr. Willoughby. Thank you for the invitation, and I'm quite curious to see what becomes of our friendship." She smiled and promptly turned on her heels to go back into the cottage. When she reached the front door, she turned around and saw that he had not yet begun to walk away. Instead, he had watched her make her way to the front door and waited to see that she had no trouble getting in. When she looked back at him, he tipped his hat and turned to go.

Many years ago, Margaret had seen him walk away just as he had today.

Chapter Eight

On the morning of the picnic on Willoughby's estate, Margaret found herself thinking about falling in love once more. Her experiment that she had hoped to test with Rupert (before she had discovered him *married*) was stalled. But now she wondered if she might test out her methods on a different gentleman.

Indeed, she thought that John Willoughby himself might be an acceptable test subject.

Margaret inwardly conversed with herself about how Willoughby might be the perfect specimen for love insofar that a relationship with him was soundly forbidden by the unspoken code among sisters. Margaret had no desire to consummate any affection she might be able to muster, which made the prospect of falling in love with Willoughby all the more intriguing. If she directed her attention toward Willoughby, she could allow herself to get a sense of romantic love, vital information that would help her perceive whether it interested her at all.

When she repeated the plan back to herself in the mirror, she wondered if she sounded ridiculous. The truth was, Margaret was rather excited by the prospect of experiencing something that approached romance, even if it had no culmination in anything substantial. Margaret craved excitement, and — like her interest in testing the same experiment on Rupert earlier — the thought of attempting to fall in love with Willoughby enlivened her.

Of course, she cared rather little if he liked her in return. Nothing would come of this experiment — Margaret only wished to have a taste of what romantic love might feel like. It did not occur to her that this was usually a venture that required two consenting parties. No, whatever love she would allow to blossom was entirely for herself. And, of course, Marianne would never know of this experiment. Marianne and Colonel Brandon lived quite far away. And, seeing as how Marianne had fairly recently given birth, there was very little chance of the Brandons traveling to Margaret's little corner of the countryside.

Before they would leave in a band of carriages to the picnic on Willoughby's estate, Margaret was still expected in Rupert's library that morning, and so that's where she went. The walk was a bit colder than usual. With each passing day, the air became colder and more crisp. Margaret liked the change in temperature, but she dreaded the thought of cold winter mornings that would require Rupert sending his carriage for her. She didn't like to be a burden, and she enjoyed the au-

tonomy of being able to walk wherever and whenever she wished.

Together in his study, Margaret helped Rupert copy out some of his new manuscript pages.
Their method was working well for them so far.
First, they would combine their notes and then
together they would write out the bulk of a chapter. Rupert would make his changes, and Margaret
would make hers. The final step was to make
a fresh copy of a manuscript chapter, but they
both agreed that Rupert's handwriting was much
superior to Margaret's. It truly felt like a collabora-
tive process, and there were times where Margaret
wondered if she ought to pull back just a bit. If Rupert could not be convinced to acknowledge her as
a true coauthor, then it did not seem right of her
to spend so much time composing portions of the
chapters. He was the one who needed to earn tenure, not her.

When they had both reached a stopping
point, Margaret leaned back in her chair and
crossed her arms in front of her.

"Rupert," she said, "what do you think of
your cousin John Willoughby?"

Rupert looked a little surprised by the question. Margaret even felt like she detected no small
amount of wariness in response to her query.

"Truly, I know very little of him," said Rupert. "Indeed, I perhaps know more of his relationship with your family than with Cecelia's. Could
you tell me more of what happened, Margaret, be-

tween John and your sister, if you are comfortable?"

Margaret gave a serviceable account of what had transpired between Marianne and Willoughby. She explained to Rupert that the whole ordeal grew to a state of dramatic climax simply because of the secrecy between the two lovers. Everyone believed that Marianne and Willoughby were engaged when they most decidedly were not. The great wrong that Willoughby had done was that he led Marianne to believe that there would be an engagement, and then when that was no longer possible, he quickly exited the scene. It wasn't long before the Dashwood family discovered that Willoughby was engaged to someone else, someone with money. This was the wrong that had completely undone Marianne. She had grown grievously ill, and her refusal to shield herself from the natural elements while going on her long walks only exacerbated the strength of her illness. She had developed a fever, and it had not been entirely clear whether or not she would survive. Margaret noted that the best reason her family had for despising Willoughby was that his carelessness had nearly killed Marianne.

But Margaret was an intelligent young woman. She understood that Marianne's decline was not all Willoughby's fault. Some of the blame, of course, had to fall on Marianne's extreme reaction to rejection. Margaret understood that rejection was part of life, and even though she had never verifiably been in love, she had enough sense to realize that rejection was simply part of the process.

Rupert listened to Margaret's account of Willoughby's wrongdoing to the Dashwood family. He nodded with interest at all the salient plot points and agreed with Margaret when she noted that it seemed Willoughby had received punishment enough for his poor behavior as a young man. Margaret felt a thrill of excitement that Rupert still seemed capable of maintaining an intimate conversation with her, even though he was now somewhat bound by the propriety of his marriage contract. She liked the way Rupert listened to her; it was like he gave her his full attention by way of his body. Margaret felt a little sad that she had never noticed this before, as if she had missed an opportunity of reveling in this sort of genuine attention.

Unconsciously, she decreased the distance between them.

"I find him quite interesting," said Rupert. "I am afraid, though, that he does not find me equally as intriguing." If Rupert had noticed Margaret's unconscious movement toward him, he did not retreat from it. Margaret was grateful for this.

"Why would you say that?" said Margaret.

"Willoughby is a man of great style and charisma," said Rupert. "He is a true gentleman. I have some gentlemanly qualities, in my opinion, but I am a scholar. My way of being in the world is different. Being a professor is part of my life. Willoughby does not have an occupation like I do, and I have often found that men who do not have occupations have the space to develop a kind of ease with life. I recognize that ease in Willoughby."

"I see it as well," said Margaret. "I think that ease is part of what enchanted my sister all those years ago. Willoughby can seem to feel comfortable in any situation."

Rupert paused for a moment before continuing, "Margaret, do you find him quite trustworthy?" There was the wariness again. Margaret could hear it in his voice.

Margaret laughed. "Oh, no, not at all! And he has told me as much. He is not to be trusted, but I think he can be found to be a serviceable friend, if not a very dependable one."

"Cecelia truly dotes on him," said Rupert. "It seems he was the one who once helped her detach herself from an engagement that went sour."

"He has told me a little of this," lied Margaret. In fact, Willoughby had told her just about everything and she had only been waiting for a little bit of time with Cecelia to hear the story once more.

"I am afraid that when Cecelia met me," continued Rupert, "she was quite heartbroken. We've only been married a handful of weeks, but I worry that the heartbreak she experienced still stings. I almost wonder if her enthusiasm for my work is connected to a desire to feel more deeply attached to me. It seems that this other gentleman was too proud to claim her as his beloved, which I find unfathomable. I cannot understand how a man would not wish to treasure Cecelia and to show her off to all he encountered. She is a marvelous woman, and she loves me with an honesty and a forwardness that makes me feel like myself — or, at least, what I *could* be if I were somehow greater than I actually am. I hope that I am able to make her quite happy."

Margaret smiled as she listened to Rupert speak of his love for Cecelia. She trusted Rupert's judgment tremendously, and she knew that even though Cecelia was the absolute archetype of a "frittering young woman" (Margaret felt badly for even thinking such a thing), whatever Rupert saw in her was good and true. She liked to hear him speak of Cecelia. It gave her some sense of what love might feel like. She especially liked what he said about how a lover might make you feel somehow greater than you actually are. Margaret wondered if the simple feeling of love, rather than the attention of a lover, would have a similar effect.

"I think you will make her quite happy," said Margaret, "and I believe she will make you happy, too. But we must find a way that is suitable for her to help with your research — the whole endeavor seems to bore her immensely, but I don't know what the remedy is."

"Neither do I," said Rupert, "but I don't want her to feel excluded. This is important to me, Margaret. I hope that you will be a true friend to me and not let me fail in being a good husband."

"Oh, don't worry," said Margaret. "I refuse to let you fail."

They returned to their work for a moment, and the sound of shuffling papers and tracing pens filled the library once more. Again, Margaret was struck by how pleasant it was to sit in silence with Rupert, even though his yearlong sabbatical had only just begun. Margaret felt that she would miss these mornings tremendously when he and Cecelia returned to London at the end of the twelve months.

"Rupert," Margaret said, "what do you think I would be like if I were in love?"

Rupert froze and gave her a startled look. "If *you* were in love, Margaret?" he asked.

"Yes," she said. "What do you think I would be like were I consumed with a passion for another person?"

Rupert chuckled. "I think, Margaret, if you were in love you would not be capable of staying cooped up in a library each morning with me. If you were in love, you would require some sort of fervent activity in order to simply manage the feelings."

"You think so?" asked Margaret. "You think I really wouldn't be able to work if I were in love? You are able to work, Rupert; why shouldn't I be able to do the same?"

"Because we are so different! Our friendship, to most people, seems impossible," said Rupert. "I am the kind of person who can be quietly in love with another. I don't imagine that you are capable of doing anything quietly, my dear friend. If you were to fall in love, there is no way for you to hide it. Perhaps I am wrong, but it would surprise me to no end if you were capable of restraining your outward affection."

"Oh, I doubt that," huffed Margaret. "I am perfectly capable of keeping my feelings to myself." Margaret considered inwardly that she knew herself better in this respect than Rupert did.

"Are you now?" Rupert smiled. "Well, then, I suppose I will have to sit in suspense when the moment comes where you find yourself in love."

"You know," said Margaret seriously, "I am only thinking of love and romance because of you and Cecelia."

"Oh," said Rupert, his tone of voice indicating that this was not what he expected to hear. "My marriage has made you think of love?"

"Yes, indeed," Margaret replied. "I believe I am finally confronting my mortality, and I have a sense that, if I wish to be married, I ought to start thinking of it now. I've put it off for quite a long time, and even though spinsterhood is not wholly offensive to me, it strikes me that I would enjoy a companion. My mother will not be with me forever. I long for someone to share a home with. After all, I have always shared a home with someone — if my mother were to die tomorrow, the cottage would be mine and I would be all alone in its empty rooms, surrounded by memories of older sisters who left too quickly. I say this to you as a friend, but I am beginning to be quite afraid of a future loneliness."

Rupert put down his pen and paper and looked at Margaret plaintively. "To be honest, Margaret, I do not think that matrimony is an absolute assurance against loneliness, and I don't know that loneliness is all that bad. Some of the greatest minds of our civilization have created incredible work in a space of solitude."

"Yes, but Rupert," interrupted Margaret, "I am a woman. Anything that I *do* create will hardly have any impact on a meaningful legacy. You know this as well as I."

"I sincerely wish that that were not true," said Rupert, "but you may be right. So, then, what do you plan to do? Do you plan to seek out a husband?"

"I'm not sure," said Margaret. "I think, first of all, I would like to have a better understanding of what love is, and then I might be persuaded to matrimony."

"And are you really so confident that you will be able to find a partner when the time comes?"

"Well, Rupert, you didn't seem to have any trouble," said Margaret. "I suspect that if I go looking for it, I won't have trouble either."

"That is bold," said Rupert, "but I would expect nothing less from you, my friend. I hope you find something akin to love, and if you do decide that marriage is what you want, I can only pray that he will be worthy of your affections... and," he added, "that he will be prepared for your moods."

Margaret crumpled up a piece of paper and hurled it at Rupert. They laughed and then began cleaning up their books and papers in preparation for the picnic. The carriages were starting to arrive, and Margaret could hear the flurry of voices in the main living areas as people gathered before their departure. She was able to distinguish her mother's voice, speaking cordially with Willoughby and his daughter Marianna. Margaret often worried that her mother was too soft, but she was glad that Mrs. Dashwood felt no restraint about showing warmth to the little girl. After all, it was not the little girl's fault that she seemed to bear the namesake of her father's lost love.

Rupert and Margaret descended the stairs, put on their cloaks so that they would be warm in their carriages, and joined the caravan that would take them to Willoughby's estate.

***

Margaret was a little bothered by how beautiful the estate was. Part of why Willoughby had wanted them to come to his home was to observe the first flush of fall colors on the trees, mixed with the lingering heat of a long summer, at least at the height of the day. It was cold enough for sweaters and cloaks, but comfortable enough in the sunshine for everyone to enjoy the lawn of the estate. The fall foliage did not disappoint, and Margaret felt that Willoughby and his daughter were very lucky to have this kind of natural beauty surrounding them. It did feel odd to her, though, that only the two of them occupied that large house with a retinue of servants.

Margaret was most surprised by the stables, though. It immediately reminded her of something that had happened when Willoughby was courting Marianne. At the height of their romance, he had wanted to give her a *horse*. It was an extravagant gift, especially since they were not officially engaged. Margaret's other older sister Elinor had persuaded Marianne that it would not be prudent to accept such a present, but it was interesting to see Willoughby with his horses now. They were all quite beautiful, and it was clear that his daughter Marianna had been brought up to be comfortable with the species.

After everyone had feasted on canapes and petit fours, people's attention turned to the stables. Willoughby offered lessons to anyone who wished to ride, and Margaret felt herself growing jittery with excitement. She was a twenty-eight-year-old woman, but that didn't mean she was averse to a jovial time. Margaret had never received any formal instruction in riding — she had never had access to a fine stable before. And so she felt that she must take advantage of this opportunity. Even little Marianna showed off her riding skills, galloping sidesaddle on a small pony. She was already a fine horsewoman, and it was difficult to ignore Willoughby's pride in watching his young daughter so excel at riding.

After no one else appeared willing to step into the stables, Margaret stepped forward and Willoughby willingly led her to what he claimed was one of his gentlest horses, an older mare named Radish. Radish looked calm enough, and so Margaret was not too concerned about trouble. Willoughby encouraged Margaret to simply get to know Radish first.

"She is quite gentle, I assure you," said Willoughby. "You are welcome to stroke her face and forehead, and don't be afraid of touching her with more than a graze. She is a horse, after all. It takes quite a lot to make an impression on her. I suppose, actually, that she is not so different from *you*." He laughed.

"You're quite wrong, Mr. Willoughby, I'm always sensitive to the presence of others," teased Margaret. "I don't ignore people easily, and I'm certainly not *careless* with them." He raised his eyebrows at her comment, obviously aware that any sort of sarcasm about their shared history would likely never subside.

After Margaret had been instructed in some of the basics, including a rather fervent request never to walk behind Radish, she was taught how to position herself on the saddle in which she would ride like a gentlewoman. Willoughby assured her that he would always be within reach until she was ready to lead the horse on her own.

Margaret, of course, thought it quite unjust that women had to ride sidesaddle — a position that seemed to make the whole ordeal of riding that much more dangerous. But she was nonetheless glad to learn something new.

While Margaret was getting her bearings on the very tall Radish, Willoughby gently led the horse around the perimeter of the stable yard, occasionally increasing his speed to a jog in order to move Radish along. Margaret was enchanted by the thrill of riding a horse as an adult. She had been given a small lesson here or there on a pony when she was younger, but she had never been permitted to ride an actual horse. Indeed, she had never had access to such a privilege. Now she felt triumphant, even though Radish was still mostly following Willoughby's commands. After several minutes, however, Willoughby made sure that the reins were tight in Margaret's hands and let her guide the horse around the yard. Margaret loved the sensation of power that accompanied riding Radish. All of the other attendees at the picnic cheered and clapped at Margaret's success, and Margaret herself let her head fall back in exuberance.

"Would you feel comfortable leaving this stable yard, Miss Margaret?" asked Willoughby. Margaret did not even have to consider this request; of course she would like to leave the stable yard — who would *not* want to leave the stable yard? So Willoughby walked over to the gate and pushed it open.

"You will certainly want to stay close, Miss Margaret," he said, "and remember that all you have to do is pull gently on the reins to make Radish slow down. Radish is quite good at following commands — you only have to be clear with her!"

"Thank you, Mr. Willoughby!" Margaret called from atop Radish. "I won't wander far!"

But before these words left Margaret's overly confident mouth, two of Willoughby's hunting dogs burst out of the bushes in hot pursuit of one another. Their high-pitched barking and rapid speed alarmed poor Radish, who immediately reared back and then threw herself into something *much* faster than a trot. Margaret instinctively pulled on the reins to try and get Radish to calm down, but it did not help that all of the people watching Margaret had now let their voices devolve into shrieks and screams. There was nothing in the immediate circumstances that could have possibly calmed Radish down, and all Margaret could do was hold on as tightly as possible while Radish expelled her fear through galloping.

When Margaret turned to look behind her, she saw that Mr. Willoughby had jumped on one of his other horses and was in rapid pursuit of them. He was gaining on them, and Margaret grew more grateful by the moment. They were now rather outside the bounds of the estate itself and were galloping through the surrounding country-side — Margaret was not sure if she was holding on tightly enough, a fear that was exacerbated as the terrain became more rugged.

And then her worst fear came to fruition: Radish halted suddenly, spooked by an approaching creek and too old to feel compelled to jump. The sudden stop surprised Margaret and flung her from the saddle, her skirts flying. Margaret knew just enough about horse safety from what she had read in novels to remember that she needed to relax before she hit the ground; if she tensed up her body, there was a greater likelihood of broken bones. What she did not account for, though, was the bed of rocks on which her body landed. Her head slammed against a small boulder, and the last thing Margaret saw before closing her eyes was the blurry face of a horrified John Willoughby.

Chapter Nine

The room in which Margaret Dashwood lay on a massive bed was dank and solemn. She was alive, but knocked into unconsciousness. If Margaret had been awake to see just how many people made a fuss over her injury, she would have been mortified. Margaret loved attention, but this kind of attention was the opposite of her desires.

Mrs. Dashwood could barely look at her daughter's face, which was covered with quickly drying brown blood. When the doctor finally arrived, he chastised everyone attending Margaret's bed for not simply cleaning her face. With the blood now wiped away, the doctor inspected her wound, which was serious but not life threatening.

"Well, now," said the doctor, "it appears that this young lady has had quite a blow to her lovely little head! I am afraid that this will leave a scar. Where is the mother? Dear mother, I wish to tell you that there is nothing to be done about the scarring that will inevitably come from this injury. Her pretty little face will be forever marred, but I do hope you will forgive me since I am going to keep her alive!"

The doctor laughed at his horrid joke. Rupert, who was perhaps the one person in the room to know Margaret best, muttered under his breath that Margaret would probably relish having a scarred face — "Anything to make her more distinctive," he whispered to Cecelia, who was very close to the point of fainting from all the excitement.

"Doctor, when will she wake?" asked a horrified Mrs. Dashwood.

The doctor chuckled. "She's had a bad fall and the impact was quite strong, but young women are hardy creatures. Her body will take the time that it needs to store up some energy, and, I guarantee you, this lovely young woman's eyes will open by morning. I have a few small fears of internal damage, and there is always the risk of fever with these sorts of aggressive injuries, but I do think she'll be just fine. She is a pretty one, I'd say!" continued the doctor. "Tell me now, which one of you lucky gentlemen is she engaged to?"

No gentleman came forward. Instead, a terrified but now also irritated Mrs. Dashwood remarked, "I don't believe my daughter is in any state to think of suitors at the moment."

"No, I imagine not!" said the doctor with a chortle. "Now then, I'll be giving her a few stitches in this pretty little forehead, and then I will leave you to supervise her through the night. I'll return in the morning to check on the poor young lady."

The doctor's fleshy sewing done, Mrs. Dashwood was finally left alone in the room with her daughter. Mrs. Dashwood was afraid of further irritating the wound on Margaret's head, so instead of stroking her hair, she simply held her hand tightly and prayed that her daughter would wake and feel refreshed — alive to the world around her when the morning came.

The other guests were shaken by the events of the day, and John Willoughby only had apologies to give to them. The picnic attendees had seen the debacle with the dogs and understood that it was not exactly Willoughby's fault that the beautiful young Miss Margaret had been thrown from her horse. But that did not completely eradicate their desire to blame him for the damage.

As for John Willoughby himself, he was distraught over the occurrences. He was frustrated with himself for ever putting poor Miss Margaret in danger, although he confessed to himself that he had no thought of Radish being volatile. He had been terribly mistaken, and he felt that all of his energy must go toward making amends for the situation. He was concerned for poor Margaret Dashwood. She had trusted him, and he had failed her. It did not escape him that it seemed he would forever have poor luck with the Dashwood women.

While Mrs. Dashwood sat vigil over Margaret, Willoughby found himself sitting on a bench right outside the door. He wished to be available if

Mrs. Dashwood needed anything, and he also felt strongly about being one of the first to know if Miss Margaret's condition changed.

It was now night. The room that Willoughby stared at from across the hallway had its door closed and was completely devoid of sound. He wanted to stay awake, and so he occupied his mind by reciting poetry back to himself silently and then counting the crenellations on the elaborately carved door. The door seemed to stare him down. He found images and faces in the designs, and, as he grew sleepier, he began to feel that the door was watching him quizzically, a whole jury of faces analyzing his once questionable character. Staring at the closed door, he felt like a twenty-five-year-old man, again forced to confront his carelessness and troubled by the degree of harm that he could inflict on an unassuming young woman.

John Willoughby felt that he had endured a great deal of penance over the past several years. He had married someone he did not entirely love, and so he suffered the pain of an ill match that was exacerbated by great difficulty in having children. Just when his late wife had become pregnant with their daughter, their relationship had begun to change for the better. They became warm toward one another, and their companionship grew to be a great source of satisfaction for both of them. It had been a strange and unexpected change after so many years of indifferent partnership. Willoughby felt that he had finally come to understand the beauty that could arise from marriage — but, just as their love had begun to grow, her sudden death upon the birth of their daughter threw him into a despair from which he very nearly did not escape.

But little Marianna had been a remarkable gift in the midst of such pain and darkness. He and his wife had not agreed upon a name beforehand, but with his wife dead and a tiny infant girl resting in his arms, he felt that he wanted to give her a name filled with liveliness. The most lively woman he had ever known was Marianne Dashwood — he wished that his little girl would possess that same vivacity. There was, of course, a part of him that wondered if his now deceased wife would take to haunting him on account of this namesake, but he suspected that the late Mrs. Willoughby understood him more than he had ever cared to admit while she was living.

Mrs. Willoughby had known about the existence of Marianne Dashwood when they were engaged, but Mrs. Willoughby was of the opinion that marriage was an economic transaction. And Willoughby, by his actions, seemed to believe the same. Although their marriage had not contained a great deal of love, they had been rather efficient with one another and with the maintenance of their household. Willoughby often wished that his late wife had lived to see what a lovely child their daughter was, but it was not meant to be.

Willoughby thought over all these things while he sat watch over the room that held the two

Dashwood women. One thing that had bothered him today was how much Margaret Dashwood seemed to resemble her sister Marianne while she sat atop a horse — even if it was only a brief flash of resemblance. Willoughby had taken some time to instruct Marianne in riding during their brief courtship. He had even been so reckless as to try and offer her a horse. She had politely declined, of course, but he had never been able to shake the memories of Marianne Dashwood on horseback. Even though Margaret was clearly nervous, she carried herself with the same open confidence as her older sister. It had surprised Willoughby — and Willoughby did not like to be surprised.

Another thing that perplexed him was the fact that Margaret Dashwood was not yet married. He suspected that this had something to do with the experience of watching her older sisters seek out love, but he also understood that Margaret was quite different from Elinor and Marianne. Perhaps Margaret had been scorned in love, or maybe she had been careless just as he had. He wasn't sure. He didn't know her well enough to make any assumptions. Indeed, when he thought back on his time of courting Marianne, he felt a bit ashamed at how little he remembered of young Margaret. She had been a child, one who tagged along as best as she could with their own romantic adventures. His memories kept Margaret Dashwood on the periphery — he couldn't get a clear picture of her as a child in his mind. It occurred to him that maybe he had never looked at her deeply enough in order to absorb any sort of meaningful impression.

The fact that he could not remember a younger Margaret Dashwood was not entirely surprising to Willoughby. He very often only focused on what was in front of him, especially when he was younger. Now that he was a father, most of his attention went toward protecting and caring for Marianna. If he ignored anyone, it was simply because he was looking out for the welfare of his daughter. But it bothered him that he had very little memory of Margaret Dashwood as a girl. It pained him to think of what his character had been. He hoped that sitting sentinel outside of her room as she lay unconscious would somehow manifest into a meaningful act of penance.

Just as he felt himself drifting off to sleep, footsteps found their way to his ears, and he suddenly saw the silhouette of a young man at the end of the hall holding a candle. At first, Willoughby thought he might be dreaming because the outline of the young man looked like a younger version of himself. It made sense that his past self would visit him in dreams, making him feel forlorn over his past choices.

But he soon realized that the man was not a figment of a dream — it was only Rupert Smith, walking the halls in the middle of the night, sleepless with his own concern over Miss Margaret.

"Cousin John, is that you?" said Rupert, holding his candle higher so that the light filled the hallway more fully.

"Yes, it's only me," replied the drowsy Willoughby. "What are you doing up so late, Rupert?"

"It seems I'm doing the same as you," said Rupert. "I'm worried about Miss Margaret — tell me, has anything changed since the whole house went to bed?"

"No," said Willoughby, "no change. Mrs. Dashwood insisted that she would stay awake by Margaret's bedside for the entire night. She asked a servant to check and make sure that she was still awake around three in the morning. I am hoping to offer that night-visit myself."

"I see," said Rupert. He sank down on the floor and leaned his head against the wall.

"Margaret is always overly confident," he said. "It is not your fault that she was hurt. It is no one's fault. Indeed, her confidence could never have prepared her for a spooked horse."

"Yes," said Willoughby, "but I should have never let her out of the stable yard."

"Perhaps," said Rupert, "but it's done now, and it seems she will heal just fine."

Willoughby sighed. They sat in silence for several moments, a silence that was only broken by the wind beating against the windows. It seemed that a storm was coming. Storms like this at the height of fall usually beckon the onset of winter. Willoughby mourned the end of the fall season. He hated winter, and yet here it was knocking against his window. In the low light of the hallway, Willoughby found himself inspecting the face of Rupert Smith, who was staring down at the carpeted floor and running his fingers over any stray threads. Rupert was younger than Willoughby by several years. He knew that Rupert was closer in age to Margaret. He also knew that they had a long and rich friendship, but he didn't know all the details. Willoughby had always had a hard time simply maintaining friendships with women. His relationships with women usually escalated to flirting, courtship, rejection, or marriage. This was inherent in his human carelessness, and it was something that he was trying steadily to revise. Nonetheless, he was curious about the long friendship between Rupert and Margaret. He wondered if either of them had ever been in love with the other, or if marriage had ever been something they considered. Willoughby supposed it did not matter now. After all, Rupert was married to Cecelia, and the newlyweds seemed quite happy with their situation.

But Willoughby still found himself wondering. Now that he was getting older, it seemed he was always wondering about something nostalgic. His age and his growing maturity made him feel comfortable enough to open a new conversation with Rupert. In fact, it was a bold conversation, but Willoughby felt that cousins could ask each other such things.

"Tell me, Cousin," said Willoughby, "were you ever in love with Miss Margaret Dashwood?"

Rupert looked at Willoughby warily, and Willoughby realized that his rash question had perhaps offended his younger cousin.

"What would make you ask such a question?" asked Rupert pointedly.

"I only know that you and Miss Margaret have had a long friendship," said Willoughby, "and I only wondered if there had ever been some sort of agreement between you."

"No," said Rupert. "There was never an agreement, as you call it. She and I are friends, and I am glad to have her support in my marriage to your cousin Cecelia. I hope, too, that Cecelia and Margaret will grow to be good friends."

"I hope so, as well," said Willoughby, "and I am glad to hear that there is no romantic history. I don't think I need to tell you that it is best to keep any former romantic entanglements far, far away from one's marriage. Certainly I don't mean to imply that anything unseemly would take place, but it is important to me that my cousin Cecelia feels secure. She has endured some heartbreak, you know, and I wish for her to be protected from that."

"Of course, Cousin John," said Rupert. "You know how grateful I am for Cecelia's affection." He paused and continued fiddling with the carpet underneath him. "And I believe you also know how grateful I am for your assistance with the leasing of our current home. Cecelia was rather dissatisfied with the cottage I had chosen. I am grateful to you for stepping in — it is very kind of you."

"I wish to see my cousin happy," said Willoughby. "I have the means to help bolster your respective incomes, and so I am happy to do it." Willoughby leaned forward on the bench and looked into Rupert's eyes with a new kind of hardness. "I know what a gentleman is capable of," he said. "I have wronged my fair share of young women, and it is my intention that Cecelia will not suffer any more of the pangs of heartbreak due to careless men. Do you understand me, Cousin Rupert?"

Rupert only looked at Willoughby. He wasn't sure if there was a necessity of any words being exchanged. There was a sense that Willoughby understood Rupert's consent to the situation, one in which he was somewhat at the mercy of Willoughby's generosity. It was not an ideal situation, but Rupert so badly wanted Cecelia to be content. If that meant Rupert must defer to her older and wealthier cousin, he would do as much. He did not think that Willoughby had any malintent with this financial hold he had over the Smiths, but he nonetheless wished that an eventual change in luck would make it such that Rupert never had to be beholden to another man again.

It occurred to Rupert that it might give the wrong impression if he remained outside Margaret Dashwood's door for much longer. He certainly did not want Willoughby to believe something about him that was not true. Granted, there had been a time when Rupert had not been entirely sure of his relational orientation to Miss Margaret. But enough reflection and a happy new marriage had erased any possibility of a future with Margaret. At least, he told himself this was so. Rupert was a married man, and for him it was quite a gift to be married to someone as lovely as Cecelia.

So Rupert rose from the ground, thanked Willoughby for the midnight talk, and then returned to his room.

Alone again, Willoughby wondered if he had been too intimidating with Rupert. Had he gone too far? Did he seem threatening? On the one hand, he did not mind intimidating a man like Rupert Smith. But, on the other hand, he did not think it entirely necessary. Rupert was the opposite of Willoughby in every way, and Rupert did not seem capable of inflicting harm on a young woman. It was John Willoughby himself who seemed to carry that particular power, not Rupert.

He returned his gaze to the carvings on the old door, curious about the state of the young woman who lay injured inside its chambers.

***

When Margaret finally opened her eyes the next morning, her mother's blurry face was the first thing she saw. It took her a rather long time after waking to fully get her bearings. Indeed, she would not fully get her footing until several days later, but she had a keen mind, and it actually did quite well in the immediate aftereffects of waking from unconsciousness.

With Margaret's eyes open, Mrs. Dashwood began to weep over her daughter.

"Oh, my darling!" said Mrs. Dashwood. "I was so worried I'd lost you — I have sat here all night hoping to catch the moment you opened your eyes."

"Well," said a foggy Margaret, "it seems you have achieved your goal."

Margaret rolled her head from side to side, trying to take stock of the room in which she rested. Her vision was a little blurry, and her head ached as if a small boulder were resting on top of her forehead. She felt sweaty and hungry, and she sensed that all was not quite well with her mind at the moment.

"Mother," said Margaret, "where am I?"

"You are currently in one of the bedrooms in Mr. Willoughby's great house. You were brought here immediately after your fall, and the doctor was called for. This was yesterday, of course. You have been unconscious all night long. Oh, Margaret, what a scare this has been for me! I cannot bear the thought of sitting vigil over another daughter's sickbed. The near death of Marianne was enough for me — at least for this lifetime. Swear to me that you will never allow yourself to be put on another horse ever again."

"I am sorry to hear that this has affected you so profoundly, mother," said Margaret, still able to access her sarcasm even through her mild confusion.

Margaret filled her lungs with air, held it for a moment, and then as she exhaled tried her best to focus on what had happened the previous day. She had been thrown from Radish and hit her head. That was what had happened yesterday, nothing more. The facts of the situation were that she had spent the night with her mind completely dark — and now she was dealing with the after-effects of so heavy a blow to the head.

Her immediate thought was frustration over all of the attention and bother that must have been wasted on her throughout the night. Margaret hated to be a bother, and she especially hated being ill. When she tried to sit up in the bed, though, she was overcome with nausea that immediately made her reach for the bowl at her bedside. Margaret retched into the porcelain basin, her insides rebelling.

When Margaret was finished with her bout of nausea, her mother quickly placed a napkin over the bowl and headed for the door.

"I'm going to see if the kitchen has anything that might help settle your stomach, my dear," said Mrs. Dashwood. "I will be back in a moment."

Mrs. Dashwood squealed a little when she was surprised by a sleeping Mr. Willoughby on the other side of the door.

"Mr. Willoughby!" she exclaimed. "Have you been here all night? How gallant of you!"

Willoughby quickly rose and put his coat back on. He had discarded it while trying to make himself more comfortable during the night.

"I'm afraid I quite blame myself for what has happened to Miss Margaret," said Willoughby. "I wanted to make sure that I could be of service if she took a turn for the worse."

"It is only the fault of that *damned* Radish," moaned Margaret from the bed. "Mr. Willoughby, why don't you come talk to me while my mother goes in search of crackers."

Willoughby laughed at how Margaret Dashwood seemed incapable of throwing off her sense of humor, even while she lay in bed with a head injury. He came into the room, and even Margaret could tell that he was weary from a full night of sleeping upright.

"I suppose you were quite worried you had killed me," said Margaret with some weariness. "I assure you I am very much alive, although I do confess I am rather strapped to the horizontal plane at present. When I sit upright, my body rebels — as I'm sure you have heard through the door."

"I am only glad to see you awake," said Willoughby. "I was worried. I didn't think that I had killed you — you strike me as rather sturdy, Miss Margaret — but I do wonder about some irreparable damage to that vibrant mind of yours." He smiled.

"Oh, no damage done," said Margaret. "Only a little shaken at the moment — and in need of a hot bath."

Willoughby pulled a chair next to Margaret's

bedside and finally got a good look at the wound on her forehead. The rock on which she had fallen had sliced a cut over her left eyebrow — the wound stretched to the top of her nose. The stitches that the doctor had used to close up the flesh looked rather brutal.

Margaret could feel Willoughby's eyes on the gash on her forehead. She did not feel self-conscious; instead, she felt curious.

"Mr. Willoughby, would you mind fetching a hand mirror so that I may assess my new deformation?" said Margaret.

He got up and opened a few drawers in search of a mirror. When he finally found one, he brought it back to her tentatively. He was not sure how he felt about being the first person to witness Margaret investigating the damage done to her face. He did not know how she would feel or how she would respond, and he worried that he would be a wholly unserviceable companion to this new revelation regarding her appearance.

Still reclined heavily on her pillow, Margaret used both hands to hold the mirror to her face. Even with her blurred vision, she was able to see just how bad the injury was. Willoughby watched her face closely. He wondered what she was thinking, but he did not have to wonder for long.

"Well then," said Margaret, "I look rather unique, don't I? I expected it would be quite worse, but this only looks like a good story."

A good story? thought Willoughby. Her face

was slightly maimed, and yet Miss Margaret Dashwood saw only the possibility of arousing future stories about the state of her face. What a strange woman! Willoughby considered that he had never met a person who could laugh in the face of such ill fortune for one's physical appearance. The fact that Margaret was a single young woman who had some beauty already only made her behavior stranger.

"You are an extraordinary woman," said Willoughby, chuckling. And then he stopped himself — it surprised him that he had spoken this comment aloud. He hoped that his openness did not offend Margaret's sensibilities, and yet he also wished that she would receive the compliment with pleasure.

"I know I am," Margaret said plaintively. "And now, with a face like this, people will never forget my extraordinariness."

"I suppose they will not," said Willoughby. "Now, Miss Margaret, can you speak to me honestly about how you are feeling? You don't look well, even though I admit your spirits are indefatigable."

"I feel…," began Margaret. "I feel myself and not myself. Everything is a great blur, and I know that my mother has spent the night in absolute terror. I almost feel worse for how she has been submerged in anxiety than the pain I feel in my forehead."

"The doctor will be here soon," said Willoughby. "Your injury is rather bad, and there is some concern about it developing into a fever, if we're not careful. Please, Miss Margaret, will you give me your word that you will be honest with this doctor? I will not allow you to leave my estate until it is clear that you are completely well."

"I'm sure I will be free of your generous hospitality in no time," said Margaret. "Now, if you don't mind, I would very much like to close my eyes for a moment... I feel so tired, John."

Her eyes drifted closed, and Willoughby was left with the shock of hearing his Christian name on her lips. Anyone would forgive the impropriety of such a thing, given her state, and yet it felt incredibly natural. It felt *good* to be called "John" by Margaret Dashwood. It made him feel that he was not so much on the wrong side of forty anymore — it made him feel younger and more lively, but not in a nostalgic kind of way. It was hard for John Willoughby to have nostalgia for his past, since he had been so carefree and reckless with the emotions of others, but to be called his first name by a young woman with an extraordinary personality made him feel that his life was perhaps not over.

Looking at the now sleeping Margaret, he realized that she did not look like her sister Marianne at all. The brief moment where he had felt like he had seen a flash of his old beloved while Margaret rode Radish dissipated when he saw Margaret helpless before him. On the bed, she did not look like either of her sisters — not entirely, at least. Margaret Dashwood looked like *herself*, like an entirely new specimen burst from the garden of the earth. She looked like a woman who did not quite fit with the rest of the world, but her difference made her all the more fascinating.

Willoughby suddenly felt self-conscious that he was staring so long at this sleeping woman. He rose from his chair and decided that it might be better to pace by the door while he awaited Mrs. Dashwood's return. But even as he paced a few yards away from the bed, he could not help but check every few seconds to make sure that her breath still made her chest rise and fall with life.

Chapter Ten

Margaret immediately knew she was dreaming. She was now occupying that strange place of lucidity that occasionally comes to deep sleepers, one that allows them to explore the stranger recesses of their imaginations with the freedom of a dream world.

But it was also a dream space that made her sense of self fluid and changeable. She knew that, in the dream, she was and was not herself (much like how she was currently feeling while awake). The dream also miraculously made the pain of her head injury dissipate. In its place, a fresh lightness compelled her to rise from the bed and take in her surroundings. She had a strange feeling that she was in her home, and yet she did not recognize any of her surroundings. She was aware that she was no longer wearing a nightgown. She was, in fact, fully dressed, as if she were preparing to go down to dinner on a special occasion. When she lifted her hands to her neck, she realized that her chest was piled with beautiful necklaces — pearls and sapphires that hung from delicate gold chains. She let her fingers inspect the jewelry, but she knew that she would not be able to properly perceive what she was wearing unless she went to a mirror.

Margaret surveyed the room — yes, it did *feel* like home, but she did not recognize its wallpaper or furniture. When she saw a vanity positioned in a corner, she instinctively moved toward it, in pursuit of some knowledge of what new finery was covering her body. It was then that she realized it was evening and that the room was filled with softly glowing candles. Margaret felt enchanted that her imagination was capable of creating such an odd scene of beauty — it was so realistic that she could smell the smoke from the tiny flames that surrounded her.

As she moved toward the large mirror on the vanity, she tripped over the oddest thing — a pair of gentlemen's shoes. She reached down and picked up one of them, smiling at how the shoe's buckle reflected back the candlelight of the room. They had been tossed carelessly in the middle of the room, just waiting for an unsuspecting lady to tumble over them on her way to her vanity. She picked up both shoes together and then placed them gently against the wall, where they might wait for their master without being trampled.

Margaret finally reached the mirror, but the woman staring back at her was not Margaret Dashwood. This was someone entirely different, someone profoundly more regal and stoic than the exuberant Margaret. The woman's hair was shockingly blonde and straight as hay — and she looked like a Greek statue, her nobility etched into the contours of her striking face.

Margaret lifted her hand to the mirror to touch the face of the other woman. But, as the "other woman" was very clearly her own reflection, she simply did the same. Margaret moved closer to the mirror, fascinated by her new reflection but terrified of its consequences. She was still mildly aware that she was dreaming, but this awareness was gradually receding into the powerful ambience of the dream.

But then there was a new revelation. While feeling the beading on the dress that cloaked her, she suddenly felt terrifying movement from inside of her, as if her insides were stretching outward through her stomach. The movement wasn't exactly painful, but it was alarming — and only after clutching her stomach did she realize that the protrusion was her swollen belly itself, full with the final months of pregnancy. Margaret gasped. She was not herself *and* she was somehow with child — what had begun as a mildly pleasant dream was suddenly transforming into something more ominous.

Margaret knew that it was terrible luck — a bad omen — to dream of an infant. She wished she knew where this omen originated. Had she heard it once in a fairy tale? Had a rather unthinking nursemaid told the story to her when she was a child? Regardless, she knew implicitly that dreaming of a baby was generally a portentous symbol. But what of dreaming about being with child? What did this symbolize?

Margaret was somewhat impressed with herself that she was capable of attempting to parse the significance of her dream *while* she was still dreaming, but this sensation did not last long. Suddenly, the door to the bedroom opened, and in walked the gentleman that Margaret suspected was the owner of the shoes.

"My darling," the man said, "are you quite sure you want to go down to dinner? You know as well as I do that the doctor recommended you stay tucked in our bed as much as possible in the coming weeks. I can always ask for your meal to be brought here."

It was John Willoughby. The man speaking to her with such remarkably affectionate kindness was John Willoughby.

"No, John, I'm fine," she found herself saying in reply. Margaret could not believe the words coming out of her mouth. She hardly understood what was happening, but somehow the body she was haunting knew very well the motions of this moment and thus proceeded without Margaret's consent.

Willoughby came to her quickly and crouched down so he could better inspect the rotundity of her quickening belly. Margaret was shocked by how softly he allowed his hands to trace the contours of the swollen mound that apparently housed their child. It was clearly a physical gesture he performed often, and he was even brave enough to slightly press down on Margaret's belly in order to search for the baby's features and appendages. Margaret felt the baby inside of her respond to the touch of its father, and Margaret's heart swelled with a surge of familial affection that she had never before experienced.

Willoughby smiled when he felt the baby push back against the skin, and then he rose to face the woman who was clearly his wife. Willoughby was tall, so as he rose, he looked down on Margaret (but was she even Margaret anymore?) before him. Margaret realized she had seen this face before on John Willoughby — it was a face of absolute enchantment and affection, the pinnacle of grace-filled love. She had seen him look at Marianne in just the same way all those years ago, and now he looked at what must be Mrs. Willoughby in exactly the same manner.

Still in her dreamy haze of understanding, Margaret perceived that *she* was the Mrs. Willoughby who had died, and she was now living out the short months before her tragic death — a death that would steal her away the moment her own child was brought forth into existence. Now one with the body she was apparently haunting, Margaret clutched her stomach with the realization that the child she carried would kill her.

"John," she said, "I am so afraid."

Willoughby took her face in his hands and closed the open space between them, folding her up in his arms and squeezing her tight.

"I have got a profound hold on you, my dear," said Willoughby, "and there is no world in which I would ever consent to harm befalling you. You are safe — all three of us are safe."

He kissed her forehead, then her nose, and then her trembling lips. Margaret realized she was crying, aware that the body of Mrs. Willoughby was not long for this world and this would be one of the final times she would feel her husband's lips on hers.

"My darling, why so many tears?" Willoughby said, smiling.

"Because I am not myself — I am sorry, John." Margaret could not tell whether the voice of Mrs. Willoughby was lying, or if Margaret was speaking instead as John Willoughby's wife.

"You are not yourself?" asked Willoughby. "What do you mean, my dear?"

"I mean that I seem to have lost touch with myself," Margaret found herself saying out loud. "I see so much beauty all around me, but I also see the possibility of remarkable pain. Don't you see it, too, my dear?"

"I see only my wife in our bedroom, her body quite exhausted since she is nearing her time," said Willoughby. "I see a woman who probably ought to consent to taking a seat here and allowing me to bring dinner to her myself."

He placed both his hands on her shoulders and looked at her squarely. "You must rest. I insist on it."

Margaret found herself sitting on the small stool placed at the vanity, and she instinctively began to pull off the long silk gloves that were making her arms quite hot. Willoughby placed his hand on her forehead — Margaret could tell he was trying to perceive if he ought to call for the doctor. She did feel hot; that was certain. And she wished for a way to immediately cool herself down. Sitting down helped tremendously, though, and Margaret was glad to feel some of the nausea slightly subside once she was no longer responsible for keeping her heavy belly upright on her legs.

But then a sudden surge of pain nearly made her fall off the stool. Something violent was happening inside of her, and Margaret understood instantly that she was in danger. The room seemed to get smaller, and the light from the candles felt as if it grew hotter. Margaret struggled to see clearly — her vision was blurred such that the room almost seemed on fire itself.

"John!" she cried out, terrified by the pain and desperate for comfort.

Willoughby looked completely terrified. He grabbed her a glass of water from the bedside table, which she promptly gorged herself on. Before the glass was empty, she splashed the remaining water all over her face, trying as best she could to cool herself down. Margaret felt that her body was on fire, as if she were burning at the stake, and the life inside of her was desperately wrestling against the heat.

"John, something is terribly wrong," gasped Margaret.

"Stay here, darling," said her terrified husband. "I'm going for help — just stay where you are. Don't move."

Willoughby left her alone in the blazing hot bedchamber. Margaret was overwhelmed with fear — but what could she do? She could hardly stand, and the life within her bid her to be as still as possible, even though the room around her burned.

She looked at herself in the mirror, but her entire personage had changed. No longer Mrs. Willoughby, Margaret stared back at herself, her reflection surrounded by a room full of flames.

She was Mrs. Willoughby. *Margaret* was Mrs. Willoughby.

The dream was too much for her — hungry to be back in the land of the wakeful, she slapped her face and pressed her eyes shut, demanding her mind to wake up. She shook the vanity in front of her and felt herself clasp a hairbrush and hurl it with all her might at the mirror before her. The image of Mrs. Margaret Willoughby shattered before her eyes.

***

"It is a fever," said the doctor solemnly, as Margaret Dashwood writhed on the sopping wet bed, covered in grisly sweat. "She will now need all our attention and prayers."

Chapter Eleven

I n the dining room at Willoughby's estate —
where Rupert and Cecelia had also remained
after Margaret's accident — Rupert looked
ghastly with fear while he drank his tea. His friend
was suffering tremendously, and there was nothing he could do to alleviate her illness. He picked
at his eggs despondently, almost as if he did not
feel it was acceptable for him to eat anything while
Margaret was entirely incapacitated.

Cecelia was jittery as well — she did not like
the dank ambience of illness in a house, and she
was also anxious to get back to the home that she
and Rupert had leased.

The butler brought a thick letter for Mrs.
Smith, and so she distracted herself by reading it
over intently. Rupert hardly noticed that his wife
was engrossed with the letter before her. If he
had been paying attention, he would have realized
that the contents of this rather stocky epistle propelled Cecelia into a state of flushed anxiety not
unlike the nervous state of her husband. Cecelia
read the long letter over five times, and, when she
was finally done, she neatly folded the pages and

tucked them back into the torn envelope.

"My dear?" began Cecelia. She was tense, and her shaking fingers hovered over the spoon she was deciding if she would use to needlessly stir her tea. "I have just had some frightening news from one of my dear old friends. It seems she has just had her heart broken by a scoundrel who promised her an engagement and now she is in desperate need of some companionship."

"Oh no," said Rupert, "which friend is this, my dear?"

"A friend you do not know, darling, and I won't trouble you with the details of the whole sordid affair — she only needs a friend right now, and I wish to be that for her."

"Of course, Cecelia." Rupert waited for her actual request.

"I wish to go away for a bit, my dear, to travel and visit my friend in London," said Cecelia. "Would that be quite alright with you, Rupert?"

"Cecelia, look at us — we are here at Cousin John's estate because I, too, am concerned for a friend. Of course you should go if you feel it imperative."

Cecelia gave a little squeal, even in spite of her anxious jitters. She immediately stood up from the table, the letter folded tightly in her hands, and then she went to Rupert and gave him a kiss on the cheek.

She pulled back to inspect his face and said, "I think you are a very good man, Rupert Smith. I am afraid I do not deserve you."

But before Rupert could respond to her affectionate words, she flew out of the dining room like a songbird and quickly shut the door behind her.

Rupert did not think much of this interaction. Instead, he returned to his futile attempt to calm his nerves over Margaret's feverous state. He was not sure what to do — how could he be helpful in this situation? He suspected that Mrs. Dashwood might need him to run errands for her, perhaps to go and fetch Margaret's older sisters, so he wanted to remain available.

It vaguely troubled him, though, that his cousin John had so much access to Margaret at present, but he was not sure what exactly was bothering him. Rupert liked his new cousin just fine, but he knew how bewitching Margaret could be. He worried that Willoughby was forming thoughts about Margaret, and this made him rather nervous. Was he jealous? He wasn't entirely sure. Added to that, he now knew that Margaret was *looking* for romance, if only mildly. If Willoughby played his cards right, Rupert did not doubt that his cousin would manage to generate some influence over Margaret Dashwood.

Their age difference was considerable, but not unheard of. Indeed, Willoughby himself was not much older than Margaret's sisters. He was also rather wealthy (although Rupert was not sure how), and he was an established gentleman in society. What frightened Rupert the most, though, was that he knew Willoughby had a good story, and Margaret could not resist the attraction of a good story. A loveless marriage that ended with the wife dying in childbirth? A beautiful daughter as a second chance at love and goodness? Horses? It was almost too good to be true. In fact, he wondered if Margaret were not in love already, whether she realized it or not.

But even if she were in love with John Willoughby, Rupert considered that this could have little effect on her current condition. The last he had heard, she was only slightly conscious, and the whole household staff seemed devoted to decreasing her dangerous fever. The doctor had explained that this kind of head injury could sometimes provoke wild and terrifying aftereffects, as the body did its best to reestablish a sense of equilibrium. Margaret's mind and body were confused at present. All that could be done was decrease her fever and keep her hydrated. No further action could be taken until she improved.

Rupert was glad to have been left alone in the dining room so he could brood. Cecelia was always so cheerful. He loved her disposition generally, but he was not able to answer it at a time like this. She had seemed quite alarmed, though, by the letter she'd received. Rupert wondered about its contents but decided that it was best not to interfere with his wife's female friendships. He desired that she feel independent; he certainly did not want her to rely entirely on him for friendship. The world was much too rich for old fashioned limitations such as the idea that husband and wife were sole companions for one another.

He looked at the ceiling. He could hear pacing overhead, and he wondered what those heavy steps portended.

***

The doctor declared that Margaret was unwell but stable, so he ordered that she be in constant supply of cold towels and dry blankets, and then he left to call on other patients in the village. He would return before nighttime. Poor Mrs. Dashwood was exhausted from all her time sitting vigil over her ailing daughter, so it was decided that John Willoughby would sit by her bedside. Margaret's mother desperately needed to rest.

Mrs. Dashwood longed to have the company of her daughters, especially if Margaret took a turn for the worse, so she begged Rupert to go and fetch them from their various locations in faraway counties. Rupert obliged, so he and Cecelia both left at similar times. She left for London with the intention of stopping first at their rented estate so she could collect some belongings for her trip. Rupert left straight for the Ferrarses and Brandons.

Mrs. Dashwood had given Rupert rather careful instructions for retrieving Marianne. Apparently, Mrs. Brandon had not yet been notified of her mother and sister's reacquaintance with John Willoughby — Mrs. Dashwood had some worries that Marianne would refuse to come, but she impressed upon Rupert the importance of communicating Margaret's dire state. There was no telling what might happen. Above all, they must be prepared for the worst.

Mrs. Dashwood was sure that Marianne would never fully forgive Willoughby for what he had done, but she hoped that Marianne would at least be able to acknowledge him and the assistance he was giving to Margaret. There might even be a possibility that Marianne would never have to see Willoughby — it *was* a rather large house. But Rupert had reminded Mrs. Dashwood that this was impossible. Propriety would require that they at least greet one another, if only with coldness.

And so the house emptied out. Willoughby even sent little Marianna away with her nurse to one of their seaside residences. He did not wish her to be haunted by the death of a young lady in her own home.

With everyone gone and Mrs. Dashwood finally able to rest alone in her own room, Willoughby took up the task of sitting by Margaret Dashwood's bedside. He had been instructed in how to monitor her temperature and how to keep her body comfortable. At present, he held a cold rag against her forehead and distracted himself from his anxiety by watching all the little beads of sweat intermingle with the water droplets from the rag.

Margaret was awake, but not present to

her current circumstances. She was too weary to speak (a first for Margaret Dashwood), and her eyes opened and closed slowly, almost as if they were overburdened with the task of blinking regularly. She did not acknowledge Willoughby when he began his shift by her bedside. Instead, she merely moved her head in his direction and then promptly rolled it back to a more comfortable position on her pillow.

She looked yellow, and her face glistened with sweat. Her breathing was labored and slow — Willoughby felt himself straining to listen to each inhale and exhale, attentive to any changes in her breathing pattern. All in all, she did not look well. But Willoughby was conscious of the fact that this was still Margaret Dashwood lying before him. If she were able, she would undoubtedly have had some snide remark prepared for his new role as nursemaid, and he would have enjoyed it — just as he always enjoyed her dry humor.

He wished she would make a jest now. It might give him more confidence in her recovery.

Instead, he endeavored to be the best nurse he could possibly be. It would be over a week's time before Rupert would return with her sisters. It was therefore his duty to do all he could to help keep the young lady alive — perhaps this would be a penance to Marianne, his old beloved, as well. He shuddered at the thought of seeing her again, although he knew he must confront its inevitability. He had wronged Marianne tremendously, but so many years had passed since then. They were both parents now, both used to the rhythms of marriage and the life of a grown adult. Surely they would be able to access some sort of understanding between one another.

Or perhaps not. Marianne was a fervent soul, and Willoughby suspected that her grudges were eternal. He had wronged her, but he hoped that she would understand that, although he had acted like a rogue, he had been mostly just a careless young man. He was not in love with Marianne anymore — this he knew for sure. But he still had strong feelings of nostalgia for their brief courtship. His relationship with her had taught him what love could feel like, but it had also revealed to him the unsustainable nature of an attachment built solely upon passion. He had been passionate for Marianne to the point where he had for a while believed he could ignore the familial and financial obligations before him. But if he had married her, there would have been no money. And he knew that, in time, the passion would have been swiftly replaced by the anxiety of poverty.

He no longer had to worry about that, however. The thought *had* occurred to him (somewhat rarely) of remarrying, especially since Marianna was getting older and would benefit from a motherly presence in the house. And it did not escape him that a perfectly eligible young woman was right before him. Margaret was older, too, an advantage that Willoughby highly esteemed.

He had no interest in marrying a nineteen-year-old girl not even old enough to be Marianna's mother. He needed someone with at least some degree of life experience. And he longed for someone he could respect. As different as they were, Willoughby had a tremendous amount of respect for Margaret Dashwood. He especially appreciated how she would try anything; he had swelled with admiration when she was the first to step forward for her unfortunate riding lesson. She was unafraid and determined to enjoy herself. After so many years of living in a state of perpetual penance, Willoughby longed for this kind of force within his own life.

And here he was, sitting watch over her. He did not think she would die — she was much too sturdy for such a fate. But he did wonder how a long illness might alter her. If anything, he wondered what many weeks of rest and inactivity (which the doctor had firmly ordered) would do to her disposition. Would it depress her? Would it make her more reflective?

He only wanted her to be well. He did feel, after all, that it was his fault that she lay sick in one of his rooms. What he had declined to tell anyone was that this used to be the bedroom that he shared with his late wife. After her death, Willoughby had found it strange to sleep in a room so profoundly haunted. He had simply moved to another room down the hall in order to escape the room's ghosts.

In the room now, he took a moment to look around at all the little objects that might remind him of Mrs. Willoughby. Trinkets and jewelry boxes were scattered across the room's surfaces, and he noticed his late wife's old vanity in the corner, still containing some of her belongings. He had left them untouched primarily because of Marianna. He had wanted her, one day, to have the ability to see her mother's things as they once were. But it had now been over eight years. Had he really left the room so untouched?

He had. And he had the ability to do so. When he felt that the room haunted him too much, he simply moved himself and Marianna to another one of their residences until the ghosts receded. While he was away, the house staff had strict order to keep the room clean but not to disturb any of its artifacts. For Marianna's entire lifetime, he had followed this procedure. It occurred to him that Margaret Dashwood was the first person to sleep in this bed since Mrs. Willoughby had given up the ghost.

It did not unnerve him, though. Rather, he liked the fact that the room was filled with new life — even if that life was in peril.

He realized that he was holding her warm hand, stroking the inside of her palm. He had done this unconsciously; it was an old gesture he had used with women before, but he had not done it for many, many years. But he was doing it now, and he felt a swell of emotion at the effect that this realization had on him.

He was falling in love with Margaret Dashwood. The burgeoning love both terrified him and enthralled him.

He did not release her hand.

***

Margaret understood that she was awake now, but the heaviness of her body and mind prevented her from performing any semblance of wakefulness. Her dream had frightened her, and she wished that it had shocked her mind into alertness. Instead it just made her feel heavier with fatigue.

She was too tired to speak, and certainly too tired to acknowledge another's presence, but she was quite aware that John Willoughby was now sitting watch over her sickbed. He had been by her side for several hours now, only leaving momentarily to refresh the wet rags he was using to keep her head cool. The silence in the room had been peaceful. Margaret understood that the mind can heal tremendously when left to embrace such silence, and she felt this sense of healing seeping into her own frenzied brain.

The silence was so lovely and comforting that she embraced it for three days. The doctor had returned multiple times but had been baffled by Margaret's silence. She seemed to be improving, but she was not yet well enough to speak. The doctor was worried that the injury to her head would result in long-term damage, but the only thing that could be done at present was to allow her rest.

If the brain was indeed in distress, then it needed all the calm and stillness she could muster.

Willoughby and Mrs. Dashwood began to alternate the time they spent by Margaret's bedside, but Margaret, in her silence, found herself longing the most for the company of Willoughby. She was interested in his faithfulness to this one task, and she was fascinated by the sense of responsibility he brought to her injury. But Margaret realized, after the third day had finally passed, that he was perhaps not simply keeping watch over her out of guilt; it might be that he *liked* sitting next to her in silence.

This attention was a new feeling for Margaret. Before the accident, she had toyed with the idea of seeing if she could feel love for Willoughby, if only as a personal experiment. She wanted to see if she could compel her heart to access something that approached romantic love — a whole world of feeling that she felt she knew so little about. But what she had not considered was the possibility of Willoughby feeling some degree of affection for *her*. She knew that he liked her as a person and enjoyed her sense of humor, but Margaret had felt that the history of his failed courtship with her sister would ultimately make the connection impossible. Now, she was not so sure.

From all the talk she had hazily absorbed around her, she knew that her two sisters were on their way to her bedside. This knowledge had made Margaret understand the seriousness of her condition, that even the doctor was not entirely sure what would happen to her. He merely claimed that injuries to the brain were infamously mysterious — there was no telling how Margaret would fare.

Margaret rather disliked all this gloominess about "how she would fare," but she did finally submit within herself to the reality that her situation might be quite grave. Her mind had not stopped, though.

And, at the moment, her mind was fixated on Willoughby. She liked him sitting next to her. She liked listening to all the small sounds associated with his presence — the occasional cough, the turning pages of the newspaper that he sometimes read, the sound of the water in the basin. He made her feel so much less alone, and it was just now dawning on Margaret that she had recently been feeling quite lonely.

Perhaps this faint loneliness was part of the driving force behind her new interest in matrimony. The odd grief she had felt many weeks ago when she discovered that Rupert was married was still ringing in her ears. And she was only now seeing that this grief was connected to the closing of a door — a door that might have taken her further away from the threat of loneliness.

But she did not feel lonely while Willoughby sat with her. After a few days had passed, he took to reading aloud to her from Shakespeare — tonight, he was reading *The Winter's Tale*, which was one of Margaret's favorite plays. Since he was alone with her, he pretended to do all the voices, almost as if he were reading to a child. This charmed Margaret, and she wished that she had the wherewithal to praise him.

What Margaret liked the most about *The Winter's Tale* was that it was ultimately a play about forgiveness. In it, the King of Sicilia, Leontes, accuses his wife of infidelity and casts away their newborn daughter. When his wife dies of grief, Leontes realizes his horrible mistake and enters into sixteen years of penance. The grief is only lifted when his daughter finds her way home and Hermione, in a beautiful spectacle, reveals that she was never dead at all. She pretends to be a statue that comes back to life when her lost daughter is brought to her. Even though she was alive all along, the symbolism of her feigned statue-state reveals how forgiveness can shock us back to aliveness. Forgiveness was capable of this kind of magic — Margaret always loved this message in the play.

It was while Willoughby was reading this play to her that she realized she was now strong enough to speak. The discovery came when she was left alone for a moment and let out an unrestrained cough. She was able to vocalize the air that her body expelled from her lungs, and the "damn it" she uttered aloud after the hard cough nearly made her jump.

Her voice and her ability to speak had returned. She did not know how the mind worked, but she felt that it likely had a sense of humor. When Willoughby returned to finish reading *The Winter's Tale*, she resolved that she would not speak until the statue of Hermione came to life in the play's final scene.

She listened and waited for the pivotal line from Hermione's friend Paulina, who orchestrates the moment in which Hermione transforms from a statue: "'Tis time; descend; be stone no more."

"I was never stone to begin with," croaked Margaret.

Willoughby jumped from his seat, shocked by the new change in her condition.

"Miss Margaret, you've spoken!" said Willoughby. After his surprise subsided, he added with a smile, "And I see you have carefully chosen your moment for coming back to the living. It's been nearly a week since we heard your voice. Are you feeling better?"

"I feel confused by the restraints that my body can put on my brain, but I do seem to feel a bit better." She shifted her body so that she could sit upright. She was still weak, but changing her position was not impossible anymore. She was mostly hungry. For days, she had been fed broth by spoon — the only thing she could keep down — and now she craved something much more substantial. But, otherwise, she felt herself improving.

"Mr. Willoughby?" said Margaret.

"Yes?"

"You have sat with me for a long while."

"Yes."

"Mr. Willoughby, I must confess to you that I have enjoyed having you sit by my side for so long." Margaret said this tentatively.

"You were aware of my presence?" he asked, now looking her square in the eyes.

"Every moment."

Before he could respond, Mrs. Dashwood flung open the bedroom door.

"Marianne and Elinor have arrived!" said Mrs. Dashwood. "What, Margaret! Are you awake! And talking, too! How wonderful — your sisters will be so relieved to see you on the mend!"

Margaret and Willoughby stared at each other in silence.

Chapter Twelve

Margaret did not see the greeting between Willoughby and her sisters. She only heard murmurs down the hallway as they completed this necessary social ritual. Margaret imagined that her sisters were the pinnacle of politeness — they always were — but only Margaret knew the subtle changes of their faces that indicated joy or disdain. Margaret was rather miserable that she missed these intimate communications when they first arrived.

She could speculate about how the conversation played out, though. Elinor was probably wholly diplomatic, while Marianne stared coldly at Willoughby for the entirety of the conversation. Margaret understood that her sisters might be staying at Willoughby's estate for a few days while Margaret convalesced — they had come so far that they were both likely exhausted from the journey.

Margaret suddenly realized that this was the first time her sisters had come to her aid. Margaret, always the baby and frequently left to her own devices, had never needed to call on them to help her with an emergency. While Margaret was growing up, it was Elinor and Marianne (but mostly Marianne) who most needed assistance and attendance. Margaret had vivid memories of Marianne's illness — there was so much concern about Marianne's frail health and its mixture with her profound depression. Margaret wondered how her sisters viewed her own current "illness," although she felt relatively sure that she was on the mend. The dream of being Willoughby's wife (dare she share this with her sisters?) had been the peak of her fever, Margaret believed. But it still meant something to her that Marianne and Elinor had made the journey.

Margaret often felt rather forgotten when it came to the Dashwood women, so she sought out attention in her own way — through her style of dress, her personality, her interests. But to have the attention of her sisters, two of the women she most admired in the world, had tremendous meaning for her. Now that she was twenty-eight, perhaps her sisters were growing to view her as a kind of equal; or perhaps they simply took pity on her because she was not yet married. In a sense, Margaret did not care. She was only glad to have them nearby and interested in her life.

When Marianne Brandon and Elinor Ferrars entered Margaret's room, they immediately flanked either side of the bed and pulled up chairs so they could be as close as possible.

"Margaret, my love," said Elinor, "Your friend Mr. Smith has told us the whole of the story, so don't trouble yourself with recounting anything."

"Yes, darling," said Marianne, "only tell us how you are feeling right at this instant."

Margaret felt so overwhelmed with the pleasure of their attention that she burst into tears. And Margaret Dashwood did not often burst into tears. She felt like a young girl again, in total awe of her beautiful and intelligent sisters, and enormously grateful to have their focus, if only for a moment.

"Why, Margaret!" exclaimed Elinor. "Why so many tears? We are here now — you can have some calm, love. Just breathe."

Margaret took in a deep breath and clutched both of her sisters' hands.

"I am so glad you are here," Margaret began. "I feel like getting knocked on the head has thrown my mind into a torrent of wild feelings that I do not understand — I need you both so profoundly right now...."

Marianne blotted some of Margaret's tears with a handkerchief and smoothed the frizzy hair on Margaret's forehead, careful not to touch the scar.

"I understand, dear," said Marianne. "We are here to help, in all the ways we can."

Mr. Willoughby appeared tentatively in the doorway and Marianne immediately froze. Margaret could feel Marianne grip her hand tighter and allow her body to become stolid and cold.

"Mrs. Ferrars and Mrs. Brandon," began Willoughby, "may I fetch anything for you? Tea, perhaps? I can arrange for anything you...?"

Elinor cut him off. "Thank you for your hospitality, Mr. Willoughby, but we are perfectly well at present — and quite eager to spend time alone with our ailing sister."

Willoughby got the message. He bowed to them. But before leaving, he sent a look to Margaret, who received his attention with a small smile.

Both Marianne and Elinor were not blind to this gesture, and they glanced at one another before turning their attention back to Margaret.

Margaret had enjoyed the brief period of warmth from her two sisters upon their arrival, but now she realized that they had many questions about her connection with Willoughby. This made Margaret wonder if she ought to feel ashamed about her new friendship with her sister's old lover. It had been *so* many years — surely it was no longer inappropriate?

For the first time, Margaret wondered if she had fooled herself into thinking that the friendship made any sense. And she also felt profound reservations about the new impulses she felt developing in her heart. She liked John Willoughby, and it now dawned on her that this proclivity was perhaps rather evident on her face. Margaret had never been any good at hiding her emotions, and her sisters seemed to see right through the now frozen expression on her face.

"Darling," said Elinor, "have you and Mr. Willoughby become rather good friends?"

Margaret hesitated. "Indeed. He has been kind to me, and I'm grateful for his hospitality after my injury."

"Oh, don't be foppish," said Marianne sharply. "Have you and Mr. Willoughby developed some sort of understanding? You obviously know what Elinor is asking, Margaret. Don't avoid the question."

So, then, the sisterly softness had ended. Now for the inquisition.

"There is no 'understanding' between me and Mr. Willoughby," insisted Margaret. "We are only friends! And, listen, I know that he was rather horrible to us when we were all much younger, but that was so many years ago! Are we never to forgive him?"

"No!" exclaimed Marianne. "What he did was unforgivable." Marianne turned to Elinor. "Of course Mother would allow something like this to happen — she was always so fond of Willoughby and *totally blind* to his faults."

"Don't speak ill of Mother," said Margaret firmly. "Remember, I have lived longer with our mother than you — she is wiser than you give her credit for, and I will not allow any remark that defames the way she has handled this connection. If there is anything outside the boundaries of propriety in it, then the fault is mine, not hers."

Marianne and Elinor were rather taken

aback by the firmness with which Margaret spoke. In truth, neither of them had been around Margaret enough as an adult to truly know the breadth and depth of her personality. They were shocked by her assertiveness, but they recognized it as mature and not childish.

Margaret Dashwood was no longer their "little" sister, after all. She was a grown woman, and she was also somewhat past the prime of her marriageable years. Whereas Marianne and Elinor had spent their twenties birthing babies and establishing their households, Margaret had learned a kind of necessary independence that did not have the windfall of a marital status. Through this time of singleness, Margaret had unknowingly garnered a degree of confidence that her sisters lacked. In this moment, both Elinor and Marianne seemed to acknowledge this difference, and they were chastened by its revelation.

"Margaret," said Elinor, "regardless of Mother's involvement with this reacquaintance, I do wish you would be honest with us about what you are feeling toward Mr. Willoughby."

"And what if I am not feeling anything, Elinor?" replied Margaret indignantly.

"You are obviously feeling something," said Marianne. "You might as well tell us. We are your sisters — we only want to help you, love."

Marianne was right. Margaret *was* feeling something. It was a new sensation, but it was present nonetheless. But was she capable of authentically disclosing the nature of feelings that had appeared only a few nights previous?

Margaret candidly and imperfectly told them the passions she was experiencing (after making sure the door was soundly shut). She told the story of how Willoughby had sat by her bedside, day and night, while they waited for Marianne and Elinor to arrive. She told them of how lovely it felt to share silence with Willoughby, how his presence calmed her. She also (very carefully) told them how she had reason to believe that he returned the affection. Although nothing had been said explicitly, Margaret trusted her instincts — she could tell that he had warmed to her, perhaps significantly.

She refrained from telling them that she had plotted inwardly about experiencing love, regardless of whether a gentleman returned the affection. It was beginning to dawn on her that this machination was somewhat childish. But, childish or not, the orientation to a potential relationship *had* helped hasten her developing feelings for Willoughby. While at first she had simply hoped to feel some romantic sensations in relation to him, she now was confronted with the possibility of receiving feelings in return.

"Are you angry, Marianne?" asked Margaret.

Marianne stepped away from the bedside and walked to the window. Margaret had been afraid to pose the question to her sister, but it seemed like the most honest thing to do. She watched Marianne look out the window, which overlooked the side garden of Willoughby's estate. Marianne was obviously considering the question carefully, and Margaret knew that her sister would answer her candidly. But Margaret still worried — had she allowed her heart to go too far? Was she selfish in directing any sort of affectionate energy at Willoughby? Was she blind to the reality of the situation? Had she betrayed her sister, if only in thought?

Marianne turned back to Margaret and inspected her face. Margaret kept herself still so that Marianne would not read too far into any small movement of her eyes.

"Margaret," began Marianne, "in all honesty, I don't know what to say. You are a grown woman — I know this — but everything we know of Willoughby tells us that he is not to be trusted. I trusted him once, and I paid the price. Have you forgotten any of this?"

"No, Marianne," said Margaret. "I remember all that happened. But Willoughby was younger than I am now when he committed those sins. Doesn't that mean anything?"

"Darling," interjected Elinor, "It certainly means something, but it does not mean that he is worthy of your affection. There is so much you do not understand about what happened."

"What?" said Margaret. "What do I not understand? He misled Marianne and then disappeared. Is that not the whole of the affair?"

Marianne and Elinor looked at each other. It was the look shared between older sisters who had a secret they kept from the baby of the family. As a twenty-eight-year-old woman, Margaret resented these kinds of secrets — they made her feel like a child again. Since she was the last of three sisters, these secrets had the added effect of underscoring her sense of continually being left out. Her role in the Dashwood family often made her perpetually at risk of infantilization, and no amount of assertiveness could entirely remedy this pattern.

"Marianne! Elinor!" said Margaret. "What is it you are not telling me?"

"We did not believe that it was important for you to know at the time," began Elinor. "You were so young, and we wanted you to maintain mostly happy memories of Willoughby. If we told you all of the pain he was capable of creating for those who loved him, we worried that we would disillusion you entirely from all the goodness that exists in the world."

Margaret looked at Elinor squarely. "Elinor, our father died when I was only thirteen, and the chief memory of my childhood was our eviction from our home by our own brother — what more could I have learned to help me see that the world is cruel? I'm afraid, sister, that I have long been disillusioned of a world that consists entirely of goodness."

Elinor sighed. "This is something quite different, darling."

"Then, please, enlighten me." Margaret folded her arms in front of her chest and furrowed her brow. She did not think that they had any ability to surprise her.

Her sisters both moved close to Margaret and sat at the foot of the bed. Margaret did not like the look on their faces. She seemed to understand that whatever they were preparing to say would likely harm her opinion of Willoughby. Margaret wondered if she would be able to actually hear what they would say to her. She had a sense that it was much worse than she could imagine, but she dared not let her mind venture to the darkest possibilities.

"Margaret," said Marianne, "you will remember that Colonel Brandon was acquainted with Willoughby long before he came to know us?"

"Marianne," interrupted Elinor, "why don't you let me tell the story?"

"Why?" said an offended Marianne. "Brandon is my husband and it is his past — why shouldn't I tell the story?"

"Because," continued Elinor, "I'm not sure you will tell it plainly."

Marianne huffed and then consented. "You are right, Elinor. I will not tell it plainly." And then Marianne leaned back and gestured with her arm for Elinor to proceed.

"Well," said Elinor, "where do I begin? The thing is, Margaret, that Colonel Brandon first alerted us — specifically, *me* — to Willoughby's unfortunate past when there was suspicion that Marianne and Willoughby were engaged. Colonel Brandon explained that the child of his dead beloved, who was then a young woman, had been seduced by Willoughby and was with child. Willoughby rejected the connection and the poor young woman was ruined. Luckily, she was under the care of Colonel Brandon, so she fared much better than other young women in similar circumstances."

Elinor paused. "Do you understand, darling? Willoughby abandoned a woman he claimed to love *when she was with child*. This is abominable, yes?"

Margaret was silent. She had suspected that Willoughby had been an avid seducer, but she had not allowed herself to imagine that he had taken seduction to the absolute limit of propriety. Margaret was not a child — she understood that such things happened among men and women, but she could hardly believe that Willoughby could have left this woman in such a dire situation. How could he have been so horribly cruel?

"And we know this information for sure?" asked Margaret.

"I am afraid so, darling girl," replied Elinor.

Marianne sat brooding. She almost smiled in satisfaction over Margaret's disillusionment. In a way, Marianne and Elinor were finally welcoming Margaret into the guild of secrets among sisters, but Margaret did not feel overly enthusiastic about the secret they had just disclosed.

Margaret did not know what to feel. This was outside the bounds of what she believed her heart was capable of. Had he really abandoned a woman who was with child? And had he also gone on to be the doting father to Marianna, with apparently no thought of the child whom he had disregarded? She could not believe it. Over the past weeks, she had watched eagerly as Willoughby cared for Marianna and seemed to treasure her unconditionally. Surely there was more to the story.

But, at the moment, Margaret was with her two older sisters, and both of them had absolutely *no* interest in hearing whether there might be more to the story. So, she kept her thoughts to herself.

"One thing I will say of Willoughby," mused Elinor, "is that he endeavored to be honest with me. It feels strange to speak of him in his own house — you understand, Margaret, that Marianne and I will not stay here. We will stay at the cottage until you are well. But it is odd to talk of him when he is perhaps only a few hundred paces away...." Elinor paused and looked to the door.

"Do you know," she continued, "that he came to visit in the middle of the night when Marianne was nearly on her deathbed?"

"What?" said Margaret. "No one tells me anything!"

"I thought that he was Mother, who was on her way to be with Marianne," said Elinor, "but it was him. Against all of his better judgement — and as a newly married man — he came to inquire after whether Marianne would live."

"And what did he say?" said an agitated Margaret.

"I questioned him on his behavior. He implied that the young woman he 'abandoned' was not entirely a saint, but I am evermore distrustful of anything he says, so I didn't think the comment to be any sort of absolution. He also..." Elinor paused and looked at Marianne.

"It's fine," said Marianne. "You may tell her."

"He claimed that he *did* love Marianne. Even as he was newly married, he announced his love for Marianne and his sadness over the match's impossibility." Elinor stopped. Ever practical, Elinor never told more than was necessary.

Margaret considered that Willoughby had also told *her* as much. She knew that he had loved Marianne, even though he had married someone else. The dissonance was not at all lost on him — and he had been honest with Margaret about how his chief concern was financial. And, in truth, Margaret did not really blame him for this preoccupation.

But she could not help but view him differently now. Elinor and Marianne must have detected how crestfallen Margaret was — Margaret had never been very skilled at hiding her emotions. It did not take long for the tears to begin to form in Margaret's eyes, and it took barely a moment beyond the revelation of these tears for her older sisters to be close by her side.

"I am sorry," said Margaret. "This injury to my head has made it so easy for me to weep!"

"You are hurt," said Elinor. "That is all. We have both experienced this sort of pain, and now, it seems, you have gotten a taste of it, too."

"You like him very much, don't you?" said Marianne softly.

"I do," said Margaret. "I am not sure if I love him, but I find myself entirely preoccupied with warm sensations that I have not experienced before. I was so worried that I was incapable of feeling this sort of affection, but it seems I am almost *too* inclined to it."

"Then you must speak to him about it," said Elinor. "You must ask him all your questions and not allow your affection to fester in isolation. Conversation is the only remedy to these sorts of emotional muddles. When Marianne and I were much younger, we believed that we ought to keep quiet about our emotions and not speak up when we desired clarity about a gentleman's intentions. We know better now. And we wish for you to know better, too, Margaret."

"Conversation," added Marianne, "can also do a lot of good at quelling some of the passion and 'warm sensations,' as you call them. My dear, the love you most need is often not the most passionate. I tell you this as a woman who understands the strength of her own passions. You are a wise young woman, and you will enter into marriage at an age far more advanced than myself or Elinor. And I am so grateful for this. You will enter matrimony clear-headed, whomever it is you join yourself to. I am absolutely sure of that."

Margaret thought for a moment on Marianne's words: *The love you most need is often not the most passionate.* She had grown up hearing her sisters speak with great wisdom, but she had never heard either of them utter something as prescient as this.

Indeed, Margaret had never asked herself what she needed in terms of love. She simply assumed that whatever species of love presented to her would be sufficient. She had needs? What could that mean? She frequently thought of romance as something that *happened* to her; but now she was realizing that it was more accurately something in which she *participated.*

Margaret asked a bold question. "If I am to marry — not necessarily Willoughby, but someone... do you think I would be suited to it?"

Her sisters smiled.

"No," said Marianne. "No one is truly suited to it, darling. It is something that we are compelled to share in, despite all the bitter qualms of two humans living in unity with one another. I have hardly had a single peaceful day since I married Colonel Brandon — but I *have* experienced a full and vibrant life. There is no time for indifference because there is always more life creeping in to all the small corners of my day. There is more poetry in this awareness than I ever could have found in my books. I suspect you might feel the same."

"I will not express myself as poetically as Marianne — you must understand that," said Elinor. "But when I imagine a partner for you, Margaret, I can only picture a gentleman who implicitly respects you. For you, I am afraid this is the only way such an arrangement will work. I have met far too many married women who do not have the respect of their husbands. And, in not receiving any sort of meaningful respect, these women quickly become unrespectable. I will not stand for that with you, Margaret. And I don't believe you would stand for it either."

Margaret was listening to her sisters, but her mind was also lingering on Willoughby. She was so eager to speak to him — all she wanted was a private audience with him so that she could learn more about the details of what she had just heard.

"Margaret," said Marianne, "I will say only one more thing for now on the subject of matrimony." She moved closer to Margaret and leaned down on level with Margaret's eyes. "Do not let your affection blur your good sense. It is fine to feel, but do not stake all of your confidence in feelings."

She paused and then added: "Put your confidence in affection that only gives you clearer sight."

Marianne touched Margaret's face gently

and then — both sisters reassured that Margaret would heal quite nicely — made their plans to leave the house at once.

Chapter Thirteen

The weather turned completely cold. Margaret had remained at Willoughby's estate to convalesce all the way until the tranquil autumn had slipped into early winter. For several weeks, she had trouble walking without falling into extreme bouts of nausea. The doctor prescribed rest and plenty to eat, which meant that Margaret was mostly bedridden during her time at Willoughby's home. Because staying upright was so difficult for Margaret, a carriage trip home was deemed too risky. So, Margaret stayed put.

She spent weeks in bed, mostly reading and conversing with Willoughby, who was a frequent visitor. After her discussion with her sisters, she had felt compelled to speak to him immediately about her feelings and lay everything bare. But her mind was distracted by her ongoing illness. She could hardly keep her focus on her books; how could she focus on her heart? Instead, she chose to use the time to simply observe him. There was still a quality of mystery to Willoughby that seemed impenetrable to Margaret, and she wished to soften that barrier a bit more.

Rupert visited occasionally, too, but he was always quite prudent in the length of his visits — he never wanted to stay too long.

On one of Rupert's visits in early November, Margaret learned that Cecelia was away in London caring for a heartbroken friend. She felt her esteem for Cecelia grow after learning that she recognized heartbreak as a valid ailment, one that required the care of a good friend.

"To be honest," said Rupert, "I have not heard much from Cecelia at all. I expected she would write to me every few days, but it seems her poor friend has taken up all of her time and energy."

"It may be," offered Margaret, "that she is trying to provide plenty of space for your writing, Rupert. She is very supportive of you — it is certainly within the realm of possibility that she only wishes to give you space."

"Yes," said Rupert, "but our marriage is still so new. It feels strange to be out of touch with one another, even for only a few weeks."

"When was the last time you heard from her, Rupert?"

"Three weeks ago. Do you find that odd?"

Margaret paused. She *did* find it strange. She was afraid of alarming Rupert but thought it best to at least continue asking questions.

"Perhaps it would be best to inquire as to whether you might join her for a fortnight — maybe you could even offer to escort her home?"

Margaret tried very hard to not let her words reveal her anxiety over what was actually happening. To her, it was rather clear that all was not right — she wasn't sure what the problem was, but three weeks with no communication was indeed cause for concern.

"You are right, Margaret," said Rupert, suddenly reassured. "I should write and ask to visit. I'm struggling to work on the book anyway. I'm lonely, you know — and I worry about...."

He stopped himself short. Whatever (or whomever) he worried about was not something he felt comfortable disclosing. The natural end of the sentence would be that he worried about Cecelia, but Margaret understood that he perhaps meant to say something quite different.

She did not question him. What would be the point?

Rupert rose to go. He looked agitated and anxious. Margaret felt sorry for him — he was a newly married gentleman who missed his wife. There was much pity to be found in such an innocent situation. She hoped earnestly that all was well with Cecelia. God forbid it be something much worse.

"Margaret?" said Rupert before leaving the bedroom.

"Yes?"

"We are close friends, yes? You would tell me if something new were to happen in your life?"

Margaret looked at him puzzled. "Of course,

Rupert. I'm afraid I'm rather indiscriminate in the things I tell you." She winked at him. "You will, of course, be the first to know of any changes. Although, if I'm honest, I don't see much of a future beyond getting my head back to full health."

"Right," said Rupert. "Right...."

He put on his hat and buttoned his coat. "Rest well, friend. I'll let you know what I hear from Cecelia."

And then he was gone. Margaret immediately felt his absence, almost as if his departure were a harsh reminder of the fact that she remained bedridden — all over a rather stupid riding accident that kept her from assisting with the book project. She had been so excited about Rupert's sabbatical, but it seemed that the world was against her taking any enjoyment during that time.

Margaret Dashwood did not like feeling lonely. But, at this particular moment, she seemed to feel a deep loneliness that had no end in sight. Even when she was finally able to travel again, she would be returning home to the cottage with her mother. Her sisters, who had grown tired of waiting for Margaret to fully heal, sent their best wishes and returned home to their families. (This did not surprise Margaret at all.)

It was while she was immersed in this frustrating bog of loneliness that Willoughby appeared in her doorway.

"Miss Margaret?" said Willoughby. "How are

you feeling?"

"Just fine," said Margaret, but the tone of her voice betrayed her true feelings.

"I wonder if we might attempt a walk around the garden — to see how you are progressing?" Willoughby was dressed for a walk and held his hat in his hands.

"I would like that very much," said Margaret.

Every other day, Margaret had been directed by the doctor to attempt a walk — either around the house or outdoors. Margaret's extreme nausea from her head injury often kept her from walking very far, but she was progressing each day. Margaret suddenly felt that she was quite ready to return home. She was tired of being confined to Willoughby's estate; she missed home, even if it meant a kind of return to loneliness.

Margaret rang for a lady's maid to come and help her dress.

***

The cold air felt sharp and piercing on Margaret's face, and her eyes watered from being beaten with the icy wind. She walked slowly out onto the landing and surveyed the garden for Willoughby. When he saw her, he walked to her quickly and offered his arm. In the cold, she was grateful for the closeness of a warm body, and she appreciated how his tall stature cut the wind.

They walked in silence for several minutes, simply observing the transformation that the first frost had had on the vegetation around them. All the flowers and leaves were long gone; all that remained were bare branches and the needles of evergreens. Everything around them looked like a palimpsest of a garden, brown traces of the verdure that once grew with abandon around the estate.

Margaret noticed a rosemary bush that still stood proudly in the cold. It would be one of the few plants to mostly survive the winter, provided it had rooted deeply enough in the ground. With her fingers, she plucked off a sprig and held it to her nose. Its balmy, sharp scent awakened her senses and her mind. She pulled the spindly sprig through her fingers, letting the scent take hold on her gloves.

She thought of what her sisters had told her about Willoughby's past — how he had abandoned Colonel Brandon's ward while she was with child. She had not spoken of this new information since her sisters left. She preferred to live a little longer in the space of warmth that she and Willoughby seemed to occupy, and she understood that broaching the topic would inevitably lead to the end of their intimate acquaintance. He had already been forgiven once for sins against her sister; but Margaret was unsure of how she could forgive the sin of total abandonment of a vulnerable mother and child. This was just too much.

So she stayed silent. The sky was gray with clouds that were likely packed with snow, and she smelled a campfire in the distance — probably a few lingering hunters.

Out of the corner of her eye, she looked at Willoughby intently. Since her sisters' intervention, Margaret had worked hard to discern the true nature of her feelings for John Willoughby. Her good sense taught her that infatuation was a very real possibility, and she also understood that she had, in some ways, brought this wave of affection on herself. After all, wasn't she the one who decided she would try the thought experiment of falling in love with John Willoughby, just to see how it felt?

But walking alongside him right now was so peaceful and lovely. She felt safe at his side, and her mind was not immune to imagining a future as Mrs. Willoughby, with little Marianna as her adopted daughter.

Willoughby finally broke the silence.

"How is your head, Miss Margaret?" he asked.

"My head is muddy," she replied.

"You feel unwell? Shall we go inside?"

"No, Mr. Willoughby," continued Margaret, "I feel that I have my health entirely this morning — it is my mind that I'm concerned about."

He nodded, although Margaret realized that he was not sure of her meaning.

"You will leave soon, I imagine?" asked Willoughby.

"I feel that I have my strength back. You've been very kind to me, but I am rather anxious to get home to my mother. I've outstayed my welcome." After she spoke, Margaret attempted to keep her eyes forward. She was rather afraid of looking him in the eye.

"If you are preparing for your departure," said Willoughby, "then the time has come for an important conversation."

"And what is that?" asked Margaret.

He stopped walking and turned her body to face him.

"Miss Margaret, I think you are wise enough to know the nature of this conversation precisely. Do you really need me to be explicit?"

She did not. "You wish to ask me to marry you."

He paused, unsurprised. "Yes," he replied.

"I have suspected this," said Margaret. "I wondered when the subject would naturally arise."

"It seems it has arisen," said Willoughby, who was searching her face for some semblance of an answer, some hint of affection.

"Indeed," said Margaret.

She knew that this was perhaps *not* the time to be clever, but she could hardly help it. Margaret likewise understood that her mind was not in a tranquil state — this was not the time to make grand decisions about one's life. And she still had so many questions! How could she organize her flurried mind in such a way that she could make sense of this moment? Even more frustrating was the lingering image she could not expel from her mind: her terrifying fever dream when she imagined she was "Mrs. Willoughby" while she slept. The dream-memory of being engulfed in flames once she saw herself as his wife did *not* sit well with her. She tried to reason with herself that this was only a dream, but there were deeply conflicting emotions that brewed within her at this moment. Was it possible to feel affection with wariness? Was it normal to feel quite wary of love?

When she finally spoke, she talked slowly, careful to offer each word with mindfulness and propriety.

"Mr. Willoughby," she began, "I am flattered by the question you have not explicitly asked but have implicitly communicated. But before I can even begin to speak plainly about the state of my heart, I must know the full story of your relationship with Colonel Brandon's ward. My sisters have explained to me that you abandoned the poor woman when she was with child, and that all of this happened immediately before you met Marianne. It seems you have wronged not only my sister, but also a poor woman in more unfortunate circumstances. And I must say, Mr. Willoughby, that I have little patience for such a cavalier attitude toward women and their children. I require a full explanation before I can even *begin* to consider the proposal which you wordlessly present to me."

Willoughby blinked at her. He was obviously taken aback by her remarks, but a look of understanding seemed to wash over his face as he carefully considered his response. Margaret appreciated how he did not immediately respond to her. He seemed to be taking his time with his reply, and he also appeared to understand the seriousness of Margaret's request.

"When I spoke with your sister Elinor, while Marianne was ill, I told her that this young woman with whom I had been connected was no saint," began Willoughby. "Neither of us were saints. I was swept up in her youthfulness, unprepared for the results of our intimate encounters, and completely blind to any future responsibilities. It also had not occurred to me that a young woman might have a rather terrifying guardian — which you now know was your brother-in-law. She and I both made poor decisions during our affair, but I now see the weight of responsibility that I carried in the whole ordeal. She was younger than me and full of optimism about her future. I found myself attracted to her youthful energy and then I sucked it dry — there is no question that I took advantage of her. After I left her, I played the rogue for a few years until I could finally offer financial reparations for the harm that I had done. Although I had already married Mrs. Willoughby, I offered to claim the child as my heir and began to pay a yearly deposit of funds for her and the child's welfare. Colonel Brandon allowed me to provide financial support, but he barred me from contact with either of them. I have supported them ever since, but they do not wish to have anything to do with me. I am cut off from them completely...."

Here Willoughby's voice caught in his throat. He was suddenly overcome — and Margaret was shocked by the surge of emotion that seemed to pass through his body, a bundle of feelings that he likely always kept at bay. And yet, here he was in full confrontation of the ghosts of his past — ghosts that apparently refused to let their grudges rest.

"I have no doubt, Miss Margaret," continued Willoughby, "that your brother-in-law, and perhaps Marianne, would never see you again if you accepted my proposal. I have learned that there is no forgiveness in the Brandon family, and I wonder if there is forgiveness left from the Dashwoods."

"My brother-in-law is my concern," said Margaret. "More importantly, my marriage is my concern. I wish to respond to you *as you are*, as an equal. I watched family matters interfere with my sisters' marriages, and those experiences were abominable. I do not wish to repeat them. I have my own, modest annual income from the estate of my late father and consider myself independent. I will marry whom I wish, *when* I wish."

"Do you mean to tell me you are seriously considering my proposal?" asked Willoughby.

"I will seriously consider any proposal that is made to me in good faith," replied Margaret.

"And what is your answer, then?" Willoughby took her hand and squeezed her fingers.

Margaret paused and looked at his face, the wrinkles more visible in the grey light of the winter sky. He looked at her earnestly. Even if this was a hasty request — after all, they had only been re-acquainted with one another for a few months — she felt that he was making it in all frankness. She was not sure of the strength of his love, or even if it *was* love, but she understood implicitly that his affection for her was genuine.

Everything was happening too swiftly for Margaret. She did not like the speed with which her life was changing — it was hard enough that Rupert had married without telling her. How, then, would she account for an engagement that seemed to shun an entire segment of her family?

She desperately needed for time to slow down. It was all too much for her. She found a nearby bench and sat down — it was then that she noticed she was still carrying the sprig of rosemary in her hand. She held it to her nose and let its rejuvenating aroma bring a touch of clarity to her mind. Willoughby sat down next to her, but he carefully placed enough space between them to show he did not intend to be cloying. He wished to be reasonable, as well, especially given the gravity of the question.

"Mr. Willoughby," said Margaret, "I am not in a place where I can soundly respond to your proposal. Your comments about Colonel Brandon's ward are enlightening to me, and I am sorry to hear that you have had no ability to connect with your lost lover and child. I feel for you — truly. But marriage is a grand responsibility, and in marrying you I would also take on the responsibility of motherhood before long. I am older than most marriageable women, Mr. Willoughby, so I feel I am fit for such a task. But my age has also brought me a degree of discretion that my sisters lacked when they were on the prowl for husbands. So, then, I intend to be mindful."

She turned her body fully to him and placed her hand on his knee.

"John," said Margaret, "I quite admire you. I am not sure of what love is because I am undecided as to whether I have felt it before — but I do know that I like you. You will have to give me a significant amount of time to consider your request. I absolutely cannot answer it now."

"Of course, Margaret," said Willoughby, "I will give you however much time as you need."

"In order to make my decision, I require a degree of separation from you," continued Margaret. "You see, I am not entirely confident in my ability to make wise decisions when I am in close contact with you. I would like to know whether love grows in distance. This is why I feel I must return home as soon as possible. The longer I live in your home, the more I will begin to see myself as Mrs. Willoughby — I must have time to remember myself before I ever consent to such a massive change in identity."

"Indeed, I believe that's very wise." Willoughby laced his fingers through Margaret's and then lifted her gloved hand to his lips. "You have not even asked me if I love you," he said. "For most young ladies, that is the first and only topic of interest to them."

"I have not asked because I don't wish to hear you lessen the strength of your feelings by attempting to put them into words," said Margaret. "I rather believe that feelings can surge through us without ever being spoken into existence. Perhaps this is my romanticism, but, in this moment, I feel it may also be a product of my desire to practice good sense."

Willoughby acknowledged the wisdom of this with his eyes, and Margaret felt satisfied with the respect she seemed to receive from him. They sat silently on the bench and watched the winter birds tumble through the open skies. Willoughby's fingers were still interlinked with Margaret's. She did not dare look at their intertwined hands; instead, she allowed herself to feel the sensation. She closed her eyes and let her fingers grip his more tightly. She could sense the warmth emanating from his hands, a warmth likely brought on by the anxious nature of their conversation. It was nice to hold his hand — and Margaret decided that she would sit in silence and enjoy the sensation for a few long moments before returning inside. What could be wrong with holding a gentleman's hand? It was harmless, affectionate, and remarkably calming. Truly, Margaret wondered why she had not tried it sooner.

"I will give you my answer at Christmas," said Margaret, her eyes still closed. "By Christmas, I will have a better sense of my affection and my intentions. Tell me — can you wait for a response?"

"I will wait," said Willoughby.

"Excellent," said Margaret, dropping his hand and rising from the bench. "I intend to stay one night longer, but I really *must* leave in the morning. Would you be so kind as to call for a carriage to take me home first thing tomorrow? I will spend the evening resting and packing some of my things."

Willoughby only looked at her. Margaret could tell that he felt some remorse at her leaving the estate. But her convalescence was mostly over — there was no need for her to stay any longer. She could handle a few headaches and a few bouts of nausea. She had stayed far too long, and she felt it in her bones.

She looked at him intently, without smiling, and then turned to walk back into the house. She did not look back at him.

Chapter Fourteen

Her bags packed and the last candle still burning in her bedroom, Margaret began to drift off to sleep. Her mind was completely overcome with the events of the day, and it seemed as though sleep was the only remedy.

John Willoughby, perhaps the gravest enemy of the Dashwood family, had tendered her an honest proposal of marriage. This was the fact before her, one that threw her mind and heart into a tumult of pure confusion. She knew that she felt a great deal of warmth toward him, but she was not sure she could submit to a marriage proposal. Everything had moved rather quickly, and the chief part of their relationship had been spent while Margaret was ill with her injury. She was resolved to spend the time left until Christmas to consider his proposal, and she hoped that it was time enough to make a reasonable decision.

She extinguished the candle at her bedside and let her eyes adjust to the darkness. She thought of the wild dream she had experienced at the peak of her illness, in which she dreamt that she was the late Mrs. Willoughby. It had felt like a horrifying portent at the time, but now she wondered if it was simply an expression of a heart that longed to be in closer connection to John Willoughby. She had no talent for reading dreams, though.

What *did* her heart truly want? Margaret looked to the darkness of the bedroom for an answer, a room that used to belong to the late Mrs. Willoughby and her husband. Margaret suddenly wondered if the room were haunted, a thought that she was surprised had not occurred to her when she first found herself here.

She tried to imagine herself married to John Willoughby by picturing the weight of his body next to her in the bed. With her mind, she traced the outline of his body in the sheets and attempted to feel the inevitable warmth that would emanate from his skin. When she breathed in, she tried to smell his freshly washed hair, and she wondered what it would feel like to rest her arm on his chest. These imaginings stirred her, and she felt a shiver pulse through her tired body.

Margaret thought she was dreaming when the door to her bedroom swung open and a man bearing a candle came rushing in. Her first thought was that it was Willoughby — perhaps he was somehow overcome with emotion and required an answer to the proposal immediately. This was Margaret's greatest fear.

The gentleman, still dressed in his outerwear and hat, came to Margaret's bedside, got on his knees, and immediately began to shake her.

"Margaret, please wake up, I must speak with you," said the gentleman's voice.

In her haziness, Margaret was able to discern that it was not Willoughby who awoke her — it was Rupert.

And he was not at all at ease.

"Rupert!" cried Margaret. "What is the meaning of this? It's the middle of the night! Is everything all right — oh my, is my mother ill? Please, tell me everything, Rupert!"

He placed the burning candle on the bedside table and then buried his face in the sheets.

"Your mother is fine," he groaned. "It is Cecelia — it is my wife...."

Margaret froze with fear. The fervor of his late night visit suggested to her that Cecelia may have died. But Margaret was most surprised by how her mind did not immediately suspect that something had happened to Cecelia. She instead had initially interpreted his unannounced visit to her bedroom as a kind of intervention, perhaps an intervention into the proposal that now hung auspiciously over Margaret's future. Now awake, though, her good sense returned.

"Oh, Rupert!" began Margaret. "She has died, hasn't she? Oh, my boy, I am so terribly sorry...."

Rupert lifted his wet eyes and looked at Margaret. He looked perplexed, and Margaret began to realize that Cecelia was in fact not dead.

"It's almost worse," said Rupert. "She has left me."

"Left you?" cried Margaret.

"Yes, she has left me for her old lover, Walter Brooke."

"No!" Margaret was aghast. What could she say at such a time as this?

"Here is her letter," said Rupert. "I received it this evening and came here immediately. I do not know what to do, Margaret... I've come to ask Cousin John to help me find her, which is something I am not even sure is possible by now."

From the light of a single candle, Margaret read the letter before her. In her flowery hand, Mrs. Cecelia Smith explained that her marriage to Rupert was too hasty and that her feelings for her previous beloved had never fully dissipated. She communicated rather straightforwardly that she had sought out love with Rupert to distract herself from her broken heart. But, it seemed, Mr. Walter Brooke had finally seen the error of his ways and had asked for Cecelia to leave her husband and elope with him to France. She further explained that her love for Mr. Brooke was of such profound strength that she had little care of propriety in the scandal she had most certainly provoked. She was in France now — no one cared what ladies did in France. Curtly, she explained that "dear Walter's" lawyers would be in touch to arrange for the legal dissolution of their marriage. She begged Rupert to cooperate with their requests. "If you ever loved me, my darling," she wrote, "then you will grant me this request and forgive me for my mistakes." She only signed the letter with a "C."

Margaret read the letter over a few times, careful to digest its profound impact on Rupert's life. She was now sitting up in bed, and Rupert's blubbering face was buried in her lap. He was distraught, and Margaret was overcome with sadness that there was nothing she could do to remedy his pain.

"I must go after her," said Rupert quietly.

"But Rupert, what if she does not wish to come home?" Margaret worried that this question would be too earth-shattering for Rupert, but she asked it, nonetheless.

"I will not be able to respect myself if I do not try," he replied. "Surely you understand that, Margaret? I could never live with myself if I did not seek out a confrontation — if she does not wish to be my wife, so be it. But I would prefer she tell me to my face."

Margaret nodded. He was right; the noble thing to do would be to seek her out as best as he was able and try to discern the whole of the situation. If she did indeed want to return to Rupert, then this would be her opportunity. Her name might now be ruined in London society, but she was still (legally) Rupert's wife. He must do *something* — this was at least certain.

"Rupert," began Margaret, "do you still wish to be her husband?"

He was quiet. The question stilled him — his breathing slowed and the tears seemed to stop for a moment.

"All I ever wished for," he began, "was to be loved for who I am. I cannot change myself into some semblance of Mr. Walter Brooke. I am only myself. All of the evidence suggested that Cecelia found me suitable just as I am. The only other person who ever gave me such a sensation was…."

He stopped himself.

"The only other person was *me*," said Margaret stoically. "I know. But we mustn't make a fuss of it now. Rupert, you must go after her. There is no time to waste."

Rupert looked at Margaret blankly. She had just acknowledged an unspoken reality between the two of them, and he was at a loss for how to respond. Margaret thought of Lady Percy in *Henry IV* Part 1, the character she loved so much for her ability to "scream sense" at her beloved. She perceived a part of her that wished to scream at Rupert: *Let Cecelia do as she wishes and leave her be. Move on. Do not beg for the affection of a woman who cannot love you.* But Margaret felt that screaming would be useless in these circumstances. He needed to do what he believed was right. He needed to find her and confront her rejection face-to-face.

"Don't say anything, Rupert," pressed Margaret. "There is nothing to say. Only go and find your wife." She smiled at him, if a little weakly, and then smoothed the hair off his forehead.

Rupert rose.

"Margaret?" he asked.

"Yes?"

"Please write to me while I'm gone — it may take many weeks. I will update you on how to reach me. Will you do that for me?"

"Of course, Rupert," said Margaret.

"And one more thing." He was now standing in the doorway, framed by the glow of a single candle.

"What is it, my friend?"

"Promise me that you will not...." He stopped himself short. "Never mind. You are a free, independent woman. I wish for you to do whatever you please, regardless of my opinion. In matters of matrimony, I doubt my opinion bears any weight."

"Yes?" said a confused Margaret.

"Please, my friend, just don't forget me."

"Never," said Margaret.

But he was gone before he could hear her reply.

***

It was a long and slow journey home (on account of Margaret's condition), but she eventually made it back to the cottage with Mrs. Dashwood. After weeks away, the whole house felt much smaller than usual. Even though Margaret had mostly been confined to her bedroom while at Willoughby's estate, she had still absorbed the massive size of the house. Now at home, she felt herself a little trapped inside its small, old walls.

She had changed, too. The injury had made her lose weight on account of a low appetite, and she felt that her body did not have the same strength as before. She would have to regain her health and the vitality of her body in the coming weeks.

This process began with scones, which her mother laid out neatly before Margaret at the dining room table, complete with clotted cream and jam.

"Eat two, my darling," said Mrs. Dashwood. "And if that's not enough, eat three."

"I feel I could eat a thousand scones and never be satisfied," said the ravenous Margaret.

"Good," said her mother. "Then eat your fill."

And so Margaret spent her first few days at home filling her stomach and then going out for walks in the cold air. She had a great deal to consider over the next several weeks. Christmas was approaching, and it was approaching quickly. She felt it her duty to think over the question as thoroughly as possible, perhaps with charts and theses, in order to have a suitable answer for Willoughby when he returned.

But whenever she tried to think over the question of becoming the next Mrs. Willoughby, she found herself thinking of Rupert. At that very moment, Rupert and Willoughby were somewhere in the south of France, desperately following the trail of Mrs. Cecelia Smith. Perhaps, of course, she was now going by the name of Mrs. Brooke, regardless of whether such a name was her legal right.

Margaret felt indignant toward Cecelia. How dare she break the heart of dear Rupert, a man who would have treasured her until he drew his last breath? Margaret suddenly felt that Cecelia was rather stupid, and she hated that Cecelia had made Rupert play the fool. Her frustration with Cecelia — whom she secretly wished to never lay eyes on again — only fueled her resolution to thoroughly consider the question of marrying John Willoughby. In her self-evaluation, she would leave no stone unturned.

But when she sat down at her writing desk with the intention of parsing out a detailed discussion of her feelings for Willoughby and whether or not they would be suited to one another in marriage, she instead found herself drafting essays on Shakespeare's women. It was as if she still felt compelled to work on the book project that Rupert had now essentially abandoned. At first, she began writing detailed examinations on female characters in the history plays — the original focus of Rupert's book — but then she thought that Rupert might enjoy reading more general essays as a way to distract himself. While he and Willoughby traveled, Margaret was aware that her letters would be his primary form of leisure. He had no time for reading books while he searched for his wife, but he certainly had time to read his friend's letters, even if they included long essays on her favorite Shakespearean women.

And so she wrote. She hoped that the writing would be helpful to Rupert, and she also secretly wished that the essays — on characters like Titania, Rosalind, Tamora, Viola, or Miranda — would encourage Rupert to teach these women characters more often in his university classes. This essay-writing also had the added benefit of distracting Margaret from her anxiety over Rupert. He sent a line or two to her almost daily, keeping her and Mrs. Dashwood updated.

Rupert conveyed that Willoughby was somewhat unnaturally upset with Cecelia. He was, of course, frustrated that she was so ruthless in her sudden betrayal of Rupert, but Rupert intimated that he was more frustrated about what a family connection to an adulteress would do for little Marianna's own marriage prospects. What Willoughby wanted most of all was to bring Cecelia home and to never hear Mr. Walter Brooke spoken of again.

Margaret understood that this was impossible. Even if Cecelia chose to return with Rupert and her cousin, her life would never be the same. The existence of Mr. Brooke and her pseudo-elopement to France would be a shadow over the remainder of their marriage. Margaret had not known Cecelia for very long, but she believed that Cecelia did like Rupert — but liking someone was not necessarily reason enough to remain with them till death do us part. Margaret was beginning to wonder if the hastiness of Cecelia and Rupert's marriage had been an absolute mistake.

When she wasn't writing, Margaret would take herself on long walks, much like the ones she had indulged in before Rupert arrived in the village at the start of his sabbatical. She could hardly believe that it had only been a few months — so much had happened in the interim. And Margaret felt, too, that her own life had been transformed tremendously.

What answer would she give to John Willoughby? She felt that she needed the advice of a friend, but her dearest friend was in a whole other region of Europe, desperately searching for his wife. She did not want to write to him for advice because she feared that Willoughby would learn of her inquiries; she also did not want to complicate the relationship between Willoughby and Rupert while they traveled. Rupert had issues enough while he searched for Cecelia — he did not need to bother himself with Margaret's frustrations.

As she walked along the moors, Margaret tried to imagine what a life with John Willoughby might resemble. She felt that they would rarely be at a loss for conversation, which pleased her, and she knew implicitly that she would be quite comfortable at his massive estate. The thought of learning all the hills and valleys that surrounded his mansion house excited all her senses — how wonderful to think of rambling about in the countryside that theoretically (if not legally) would belong to her!

Margaret also thought of Marianna Willoughby, a young girl who had experienced the whole of her life thus far without a mother. Margaret did not believe that marrying Willoughby for the purpose of giving Marianna a mother was a suitable reason on its own, but she nonetheless found it compelling as a consequence of accepting his proposal. Margaret felt that she would enjoy skipping those earlier years of motherhood and going straight to caring for a *child*. There was, of course, the possibility that Margaret and Willoughby would have children of their own. This was an element of matrimony that actually gave Margaret a great deal of pause. She had watched her sisters stay perpetually with child for nearly all of their marriages — there never seemed to be a moment in which Marianne or Elinor were not either with child or nursing a child. Margaret understood that this was a rather straightforward component of married life, but it still unnerved her. She had spent so many years enjoying the independence of only caring for herself; the thought of introducing a way of life that necessitated the care of another more vulnerable being made her anxious.

Perhaps she was overthinking this. She wondered how many women throughout history belabored the points that ran through her mind over the question of matrimony — was she actually quite alone in her frustrated analysis?

Then there was also the question of family relationships. Margaret knew that marrying John Willoughby would likely create a temporary fissure in her relationship with the Brandons. Her brother-in-law would perhaps lead the charge on keeping his family distant from Margaret for a while, but she knew that he cared for her deeply as an adopted younger sister. There would be a few rough years, but he would probably forgive her in time.

More importantly, Margaret understood that such a marriage would completely alter her relationship to Marianne. Marianne was a mature woman now; though she disliked Willoughby for his past sins, she would not begrudge Margaret marrying a man for love, even if it was a man who once wronged Marianne herself. As with Colonel Brandon, there would be a season of distance, but it would all work out in the end.

The chief obstacle to the match, then, was Margaret's own will. Did she *want* to be married to Willoughby? Could she envision herself as a true partner to him?

Margaret had been correct in thinking that a good deal of distance would do her mind good — she was resolved to not make a hasty decision. For so long, she had had little to no interest in being married. Now, the thought seemed to consume her. Her days consisted of thinking about marrying Willoughby, worrying about Rupert, and writing essays to send out to Rupert in the French countryside. She hoped that he did not simply throw them away; after all, she was not keeping any copies of her writing. She only meant to soothe him with words that were wholly unrelated to the matrimonial mess in which he found himself.

But, even with the distance, she could not help muse on what it had been like to have Willoughby by her bedside for all those weeks. His presence had calmed her, and her affection for him had grown in the midst of warm and meaningful silence.

She thought that it might be quite nice to grow old with someone who could be richly present with her, even without words.

Chapter Fifteen

Weeks passed. It was now December, and the daily dispatches from Rupert had grown grave and indifferent. The letters revealed that Cecelia was quite resolved to her decision, and Rupert felt that it would be inhumane of him to insist that she return with him. Most of all, he was rather overwhelmed by the requests of Mr. Walter Brooke's lawyer, who seemed intent on dissolving the marriage as soon as possible. Legal divorce was hard to come by in England, but Mr. Brooke appeared to have financial resources that made anything possible. Poor Rupert felt that he had little choice in the matter — but, most of all, he did not wish to be married to someone who shunned him. In that sense, the decision was relatively easy.

Margaret began to anticipate his return, although she did not expect him to stay long. Why would he want to return to a home that housed the memories of his too-short marriage?

The visit finally came rather late at night in mid-December. There was snow on the ground, and the full moon reflected white, glowing light onto the face of the cottage. Margaret and Mrs. Dashwood were having their after-dinner tea by the fireplace when they heard the reluctant knock at the door.

It was Rupert. Alone.

With his clothes laced with wet snow, he entered the parlor and bowed to both Margaret and Mrs. Dashwood. Margaret immediately knew the outcome of his journey to France, and so she stood up directly to embrace his cold body.

"It is finished, isn't it?" whispered Margaret as she held Rupert.

Rupert laid his head on her shoulder — they were similar in height — and said, "It is — she would not return with me. I am alone now."

Margaret pulled back from her friend. "Oh, Rupert, I know you are in great pain at present, but you are certainly not alone."

Mrs. Dashwood, aware that Margaret and Rupert might wish to talk in private, rose to go. Before leaving for the kitchen, she patted Rupert on the arm and gave him a pitying look.

"Margaret," implored Rupert, "don't you understand? I proved so unworthy of being a husband that I could barely keep a wife for more than a month. I cannot express to you how abominable I feel. Women have rejected me plenty of times in my own pursuits of love, but never have I been both accepted and rejected within the *same season*. What will I tell my parents, Margaret? They know nothing of this. They are already disappointed that

I became a professor and not a lawyer — how will they be able to bear this failure of their son? Oh God, and the estate — I'll have to give it up. But it's no matter. It was much too lush for me. There is no way Willoughby will help anyhow now that we are hardly connected in law...."

"Rupert, what do you mean by that?" said Margaret.

"I suppose you would have discovered it eventually," replied Rupert. "There is no way I could have afforded the estate Cecelia and I were leasing on my professor's salary. Cecelia would not submit to living anywhere smaller — so Willoughby stepped in and paid the difference. I will have to leave immediately, I believe. But do not worry about that, Margaret. You, of all people, know that I will be much happier in humbler circumstances."

Margaret felt a lump develop in her throat.

"I will return to London, back to my old quarters near the university," said Rupert, as if to reassure himself that he would be alright.

"Rupert, please," said Margaret, "won't you sit down and rest a moment?"

He nodded and sat on an old wooden chair, careful not to get any of the nicer couches wet with his snow-drenched clothes.

"I feel as though we've changed places," mused Rupert. "Do you remember when Cecelia and I arrived, and you entered this very parlor sopping wet from the storm?"

"Yes, I remember," Margaret said, smiling.

"I was so afraid to introduce you to Cecelia," he said. "I knew you would be angry with me for not warning you, but I didn't know how to broach the subject."

"It does not matter anymore, Rupert," she said. "You are my friend, and I could not help but be happy for you — just as I cannot help but feel pain for you right now."

"Margaret, when you met Cecelia, did you think I had made a poor decision?" He was asking her honestly, but Margaret was not entirely sure how honest she could be in return.

"I felt she was…." Margaret hesitated. "I felt she was rather young. But, you see, I am getting rather old — so perhaps everyone seems young to me now, at least among those who are getting married."

"And what else," said Rupert. He was not so much asking as prompting her to continue. He seemed to know that she had much more to say.

"To be quite honest, Rupert," she continued, "I wondered what the two of you would converse about. She appeared to be enchanted with you, but I suspected that such rapture would not sustain you through a lifetime of conversations over breakfast and coffee."

"It often did not matter what we talked about," said Rupert. "What I enjoyed the most was her company — everything seemed to be such a cause for delight for Cecelia, and I only wanted to better learn her optimistic way of being in the world. It never occurred to me that she would cease to be delighted with me."

"And yet that appears to be what happened," said Margaret gravely. "This is my distrust of marriage, Rupert — it is perhaps the chief reason why I struggle to submit to the idea of matrimony. My interest is often leaping about from one thing to another. How on earth could I be held responsible for keeping my interest to a single person — and for the rest of my life?" Margaret was thinking specifically of the fluidity of her interest between John Willoughby and, yes, Rupert Smith. And the emotion was only magnified now that Rupert was standing before her.

Rupert contemplated the question before answering. Margaret could see on his face that he had thought about this topic quite a lot over the past several weeks. Indeed, he had been confronted with the reality of human frailty and of the variability of love's attention.

"It is absolutely human to have a wandering interest, whether in subjects or in people," said Rupert. "But I suppose I am of the belief that one's choice in a spouse offers the stability of an honest and open connection. Fidelity matters, of course, but I had hoped that my wife and I could enjoy deep honesty with one another. It occurs to me that Cecelia never felt comfortable being honest with me; otherwise, she might have told me of her feelings long before we entered into a compact of marriage. Truly, the only area in which I fault her is in her reluctance to speak plainly with me."

Margaret considered his words carefully. She felt that he was right; honesty had the potential to feel like home. And it seemed that Cecelia never quite reached that place of comfort with Rupert, even though she had agreed (quite heartily) to become his wife.

She had never seen Rupert like this before. They had shared plenty of meaningful conversations over the course of their friendship, but never had the subject of their discourse been so grave. Margaret felt rather in awe of the wisdom Rupert had acquired from a few months of marriage and a horrible betrayal from his estranged wife. She knew that suffering often produces great wisdom in a person, but she had not expected to see it in her dearest friend.

"Rupert," said Margaret, "I am sorry for what has happened. There is nothing I could say to alleviate your pain, and I know you realize this fact as well. But I wish you to know that my friendship to you is unceasing. You could marry five more times and all of them end in scandal, and I do not believe it would matter to me. You know this, do you not? You know that I will never stop being your friend?"

Rupert smiled and reached over to take her hand.

"You are an extraordinary person, Margaret Dashwood," he said.

Margaret was grateful that he had chosen to use the word *person* instead of *woman*. She would much rather be extraordinary for her personhood, not simply for her womanly traits.

"I'm glad you think so." Margaret squeezed his hand.

"I must go back to the estate and begin packing," continued Rupert, rising as he spoke. "I intend to return to London as soon as possible. I cannot stay here."

"No, I suppose you cannot," replied Margaret. "Will you try and continue working on the book while you finish out your sabbatical?"

"Perhaps," he said. "We shall see. I've rather liked reading your essays on the women — I'm grateful to you for trying to occupy me while my world was crumbling, Margaret."

"Of course," she said.

"I'd love to read more, if you feel up for it," he said. "Perhaps we ought to write a book together anyway. I'd like that a great deal."

Margaret's heart swelled. "I would like that, too. But you should rest first."

"Yes, indeed." He moved to the entryway. "Please give your mother my regards, but I must be going."

"Godspeed, Rupert," said Margaret. "Write soon."

"Always."

And then he was gone.

***

Christmas was near, and Margaret felt sure that Willoughby would desire an answer as soon as possible. She had to make a decision, and she needed to be *resolved* that the decision was the right one. Margaret had been single long enough to know that marriage proposals were not rampant for an independently minded woman such as herself, so it was important that she mindfully consider this offer. It was possible that another proposal might be long in coming, if it came at all.

Mostly, Margaret confronted her insufferable silliness before Rupert had arrived for his sabbatical. She had led herself to believe that she could compel herself to experience feelings of love, and she believed that she could generate them through a scientific process of emotional experimentation. She could not have been more wrong. If there was anything she had learned over the past many months, it was that love was not prone to experimentation; in fact, it was resistant to it. There was no experiment Margaret could possibly devise to assess romantic feelings in a predictable and rational way. Her feelings for Willoughby did not strike her as rational; they simply existed, and therefore must be addressed.

Her distance from Willoughby had been very instructive. Time apart had given her some semblance of clarity, although her strong feelings of infatuation toward him nonetheless clouded her judgement when she lingered too long on such thoughts. The truth was that John Willoughby rather took her breath away, but Margaret was not convinced that this was reason enough to join herself to him for life.

She had so many questions. Rupert had spoken profound truth when he spoke of matrimony as a place of deep honesty. Margaret was unsure of whether she could achieve such honesty with Willoughby. Willoughby even claimed himself that he was not to be trusted — perhaps she ought to take him at his word.

There came a point in all her musings where she realized she had gone over the subject so thoroughly that there was perhaps nothing more to consider. Now all she could do was trust her instincts when the time came to give him an answer.

On Christmas Eve, Margaret found herself inclined to stay away from the cottage. She had a strong sense that Willoughby would likely attempt to call, and she decided that the best remedy to her anxiety was to get herself as far from the cottage as her legs could take her. She decided she would attempt the walk to the small house that Rupert first indicated he would lease during his sabbatical, the house that Cecelia had rejected because it was not grand enough for her taste. Margaret had practiced this walk several times before Rupert and Cecelia arrived. She had been quite confident that it would be a daily journey for her, so she had longed to get used to it. None of that mattered now, of course, but this path somehow felt like the natural walking venture for a day like

Christmas Eve — a day filled with expectancy and hope.

It was cold, but the snow had halted for a few days. Margaret's boots moved easily over the moderate layer of smooth snow. She could feel her legs burning with exercise, but this only motivated her to move more. She was glad to be active and outside. The thought of waiting in the cottage all day for a call from Willoughby was unbearable to her.

Margaret Dashwood, of course, waited for no one — *especially* not a gentleman.

And so she walked. When she finally reached the tall hill that overlooked the small farm attached to the house that Rupert once planned to lease, she felt her heart sink over the reminder that it had never been occupied by her friend. It was empty now, too. She had heard that only a caretaker tended to the crops and animals, but the house was still without a tenant.

Margaret thought that Rupert would have loved to live in such a quaint establishment as this one. Even under a blanket of snow, it looked tranquil and romantic — like something out of a poem. She imagined how easy it would have been for them to work in such beautiful surroundings. It was not that the larger estate he had rented with Cecelia was not beautiful; it was only that it did not seem to match the personality of her dear friend. He was a humble scholar, not a high-minded member of the landed gentry.

By now, Rupert was home in London. He wrote that he intended to spend his Christmastide alone. He did not believe that celebrating was worthwhile, especially since this would have been his first Christmas with Cecelia. He hoped that the holiday would pass quickly and without any significant clamor. Margaret understood that this was probably best, but she still wished that he would at least spend his holiday among good friends.

Margaret surveyed the small farm and wondered how charming it would be if it were outfitted for the Christmas holiday. Just imagining it made her feel warm inside.

Suddenly, Margaret heard the sound of a horse's hooves cantering up behind her. When she turned around, she saw John Willoughby, riding none other than Radish. He slowed Radish's pace as they approached Margaret, and then he swung to the ground. Radish immediately began to nose around in the snow, looking for any shoots of hay that remained from the harvest.

"I see you have found me," said Margaret, eying Radish warily.

"I thought it only appropriate that I bring along Radish so that she might finally beg your forgiveness," smiled Willoughby.

Margaret smiled in return. She knew exactly what he was here for, but she was not sure she could bring herself to initiate the subject. Instead, she attempted to make conversation.

"Do you see that farm at the bottom of the hill?" said Margaret. "This was the original small estate that Rupert was to lease for his sabbatical. At first, I wondered why Cecelia did not find it suitable. It is a perfectly charming establishment. But now, of course, I see that it was Rupert she was not fully attached to, not where they lived."

"It is a fine little house down below," said Willoughby, "but I agree with Cecelia that it was not at all suited to her station in society."

"But she was a professor's wife," argued Margaret. "What could have been more suitable than this?"

Willoughby scoffed. "I'd rather not speak of the former Mrs. Smith, if you don't mind. It brings me too much pain."

"More pain than Rupert?"

"Of course not," said Willoughby, "but I rather wish Cecelia had been more discerning in her choices. I shudder to think what this scandal will do for my Marianna's standing in society. A sordid event such as this one does not quickly leave the minds of society's elite. I wonder if they will ever forget."

"Do you not feel pity for Cecelia?" asked Margaret. "After all, she is the one who now must continue her life with a ruined reputation. I do not like her, but I must say I applaud the boldness of her honesty."

"You applaud her?" said a confused Willoughby. "Why on earth would you ever *applaud* her?"

"Oh, that's quite simple," said Margaret. "She found that she had made a poor decision in her match with Rupert and that she did not love him. So, instead of spending the rest of her life attempting to live a lie, she took action and changed her circumstances. Yes, there were horrible consequences that she would inevitably endure, but she ultimately played an active role in her own destiny. I am certainly disappointed with how she wronged my friend, but I cannot deny the power of her autonomy in this situation. How many women remain in marriages that they are not suited to — no matter how kind the husband — to avoid a lashing from high society? The end of a marriage is a blight on one's life, but I wonder if, at times, it is the only mechanism for cultivating true honesty between former lovers. Perhaps the former Mrs. Smith made her vows to Rupert in earnest. But I must admit, I have lived long enough to know that one's commitment to promises can change. And my experience of you, John, is that you also understand the changeability of vows."

She had made him uncomfortable. It had not been Margaret's intention, but she saw that her words had propelled him into a state of discomfort. It became clear to her that Willoughby had no corner of his mind that was amenable to forgiving his cousin. Indeed, she began to wonder if he had abandoned her completely.

"Are you still in touch with your cousin Cecelia?" Margaret asked carefully.

"No," he said. "I have resolutely cut off all contact with the former Mrs. Smith. I wish her to have no part of my family, for fear of her decisions corrupting my child. Surely, Miss Margaret, you understand why I must do so? Cecelia is ruined — there is nothing to be done, even when she does legally marry Mr. Brooke. The blight of her poor decisions will carry her everywhere."

"John," Margaret pressed, intent on continuing to use his Christian name, "but do you not see that calling her 'ruined' is hypocritical? Are you not guilty of the same poor behavior in your own past?"

"That was entirely different," he replied. "Although my behavior with Colonel Brandon's ward, and with your sister Marianne, was reprehensible, I never went so far as to legally bind myself to either of them."

"But you have a child with your first lover," said Margaret.

"Yes," he said curtly, "and I have done my duty by both mother and child."

"So, then," continued Margaret, "do you feel yourself absolved? Do you not feel that your own life bears a quality of 'ruin,' as you call it?"

"Life is quite precious," he replied, "and what kind of example would I be to Marianna if I lived as if my existence were ruined entirely by the sins of my youth?"

"I see...," said Margaret.

She was not sure what to say next. The reason for his visit to her on the hillside was to inquire after her answer to his proposal of marriage, but the main topic had not yet been brought forth.

"Margaret, please," he said, "can we cease talking of such horrid matters? Would it help for you to know that I feel great pain at the loss of Cecelia? She was dear to me, but her decisions have placed a rift between us that I feel rather incapable of traversing. She has made her decision and is now on her own — there is nothing for me to do for her."

Margaret silently thought of *many* things that he could do for her, but she kept them to herself. The purpose of their meeting was to discuss marriage, not to gossip about Cecelia and her new life with Mr. Walter Brooke.

"My darling Margaret," he began. "Today is Christmas Eve."

"I am aware of the date," she replied.

"Please don't tease me," said Willoughby. "I think you know that I am here before you in earnest. I come to hear your answer. I wish to know if you could love me and be my wife."

Margaret felt her heart swell with emotion toward the man standing before her, a sensation that clouded her logic and made her uneasy on her feet. She saw his capacity for great honesty and vulnerability in asking if she could love him, and it charmed her. The surge of feelings almost made her forget the harshness with which he had just spoken of Cecelia, a harshness that made Margaret question whether she knew this man at all. But to see him now, with all of the affection of his heart apparently directed toward her, made Margaret wonder how she could ever deny him her hand.

Margaret intended to behave rationally during this conversation, however, and so she did her best to keep those strong feelings at bay. She needed all of her reason right now.

What did her reason tell her? As she had gotten older, she grew to understand that reason often did not speak plainly — or even in a language she understood. At this moment, all she had was herself, and she needed to decide how she would answer the dashing, flawed human being who stood before her.

"Dear Margaret," said Willoughby, "don't you recognize that, in you, I see a kind of redemption? I will not mince words about it. In marrying you, I seek to restore the innocence I once had. I have a deep sense that only you are capable of granting me that restoration."

She considered his words and then replied plainly: "It would make a lovely story of redemption for me to marry you, don't you think? Like something out of a novel. How interesting, though, that the gentleman — if he attempts penance — will nearly always be redeemed. I'm afraid I have never read a novel that offered such a gracious ending to a woman."

"No, I suppose not," said Willoughby, who

was growing quite confused. "But I don't claim to be a great reader of novels. I much prefer poetry."

"Of course," said Margaret. "I wonder, John, about your capacity for forgiveness. I don't mean to be rude, but I wish to make sure that we make this decision with a full sense of one another's faculties. I have never been married, but I am of the belief that it includes a great deal of grace. If I were to wrong you, I wonder if you would forgive me?"

"Certainly I would forgive you," said Willoughby.

"But what is the limit of the wrong I could do to you before your forgiveness runs out?" she asked.

"Margaret," he implored, "why do you insist upon being so scientific about such things? Is it not enough to say that, if you wronged me, I would endeavor to forgive you? If you were my wife, and you begged my forgiveness for an unthinkable sin, then would it not be within the realm of my vows to try and forgive you?"

Margaret loved his words. But she was unsure of whether she could trust them. And, yet... she loved his words.

Before offering her final answer, she approached him slowly, brushed his scarf away from his neck, and kissed him on the smooth skin under his ear.

Chapter Sixteen

Miss Margaret Dashwood did not like waiting, but the reality of the natural world necessitated that, every year, she must wait patiently for the harshness of an English winter to eventually give way to spring. She disliked the metaphor in novels about a heroine being in the "autumn" of her life, a designation that certainly would have been thrown upon Margaret were she a fictional character. The metaphor was not sustainable, though; autumn gave way to winter, which gave way to spring. One did not remain among the golden, fallen leaves forever. If you survived the winter, you got the reward of spring.

Margaret and Mrs. Dashwood spent the long winter huddled in the cottage, only leaving for a fortnight at the home of each older sister. It was a peaceful period, marked by plenty of reading and tea-sipping (enriched with brandy). Margaret was glad for the company of her mother — as time passed and Margaret became older, she was able to enjoy the friendship of Mrs. Dashwood, as opposed to only viewing her as a maternal presence. It was a lovely season of life, and Margaret was intent upon soaking it up while it lasted.

She understood implicitly that it would not last long. Margaret knew that her life was about to change tremendously, and this winter was the hibernation period before all was altered forever.

Her mother, in fact, knew nothing about what had transpired with Willoughby. Margaret preferred it that way. She felt that Mrs. Dashwood had been too involved in the marriage process of Elinor and Marianne — and Margaret hoped to keep a small corner of her mind, especially as pertains to marriage, all to herself.

When the first buds of spring began to make their appearance in the garden, Margaret could have wept. The tiny baubles of green that appeared on decrepit twigs filled her with a sense of hopefulness about how her life would be a constant cycle of renewal. Her twenty-ninth birthday had come and gone in the darkness of winter, but she felt no qualms about the passing years. She *liked* getting older, and she appreciated how the past year of her life had brought her a new understanding of the pain and joy that humans could inflict upon one another.

She had watched her dearest friend marry and then experience the heartbreak of betrayal. She had experienced something that approached romantic love — although she still wondered at its meaning. And she had found herself on the brink of marriage with a proposal from the most unexpected of gentlemen.

Indeed, Margaret Dashwood knew that she would be married by the conclusion of spring.

She kept this information to herself, of course, for fear of arousing any unnecessary clamor from her mother. Margaret wished to prepare for marriage in solitude. The inner workings of her heart and mind required space for contemplation. For a woman who had been independent for so long, and who had nearly thrown aside all expectations of marriage, the preparation for entering into a state of matrimony was rather intense. In all of her time alone, she considered what she had said to Rupert over a year ago when asked about her own philosophy of marriage: the inevitability of two people becoming lovers, if mutual affection is truly present. She was beginning to realize that she had spoken with wisdom, even in spite of her lack of experience. Margaret understood this inevitability and even felt herself grow to embrace it. It did not feel like an upheaval of her independence to accept the forces of fate, even if her fate was marriage; it felt like an opportunity to allow fate to extend her a kind of grace.

Margaret was now daily training her mind to consider what living in partnership with another might feel like. She must cease to think only of herself — although she roundly rejected claims from preachers who said that wives ought to throw aside *all* thoughts of themselves for the sake of their husband and children. Margaret knew that she could never fully cast aside herself. In the end, all she *had* was herself; to reject it would be entirely irresponsible.

Even Mrs. Dashwood seemed to notice that a change had come over Margaret, although she acknowledged it silently. Margaret wondered what would happen to the cottage once she married and moved away. Her mother would not do very well living alone. Likely, she would move in with Marianne and Colonel Brandon — they had space enough for the addition of a mother-in-law. The cottage would probably be leased to someone else.

It made Margaret feel strange to imagine another family living in her home. She had lived in this house since she was thirteen years old. The majority of her life had been spent within its old walls. She had watched the women in her family have their hearts broken and then restored, all within the confines of the cottage. It was odd to think of the romantic ghosts that haunted this place. To eventually abandon it felt like a kind of profound injustice against the memories the house held sacred.

But she understood that she *would* leave it. In a way, she realized that she would never become the next version of Margaret Dashwood if she did not find a way to move on from the home that fostered her. Her progress was inevitable.

It was strange to imagine herself married, but she felt that it only made her vision of herself grow grander. She could see how love was not built upon scarcity, but upon abundance. As she leaned into the mechanism of love, her personhood grew. She would grow as she loved a partner and loved children; and, in growing, she would only become more acquainted with herself.

At least, this is what she hoped for. She thought once more about how Rupert had asked her how she would describe her philosophy of marriage. She had offered a serviceable answer at the time. Now she understood that she would never be able to articulate such a philosophy *in its entirety* unless she were actually married. There is no worth in philosophy that detaches itself from the conditions it seeks to examine. She could not philosophize fully about such things unless she agreed to them herself.

She could say one thing about marriage, however, even though she had yet to experience it. Against all claims to the contrary, it was not as secure an institution as one might be led to believe. The daily challenge of marriage, Margaret suspected, was the faithful attempt to manifest that security through one's actions. It was less a vow than a practice.

And she felt rather ready to begin.

***

In early April, Margaret found herself removing her shawl while she worked in the garden — the sun had finally grown warm enough to announce the true beginning of springtime. The sky was splattered with clouds, and Margaret felt a lovely sense of peace while she pulled away the dead weeds that had surrounded the stems of her rose bushes. She heard her mother humming an old folk song through the open kitchen window. Quietly, she hummed along while tossing aside the mulch.

In her periphery, she saw the outline of a gentleman making his way up the steep hill that led to the cottage. Margaret leaned back on her ankles and focused her vision so she could discern the identity of her visitor. Seeing Margaret in the garden, the gentleman changed his course, skipping the front door and coming straight for the garden. The bright sun was behind him, and he looked to Margaret like a shadow emerging from an ocean of light.

"I wondered when you would come," said Margaret cheerfully.

The gentleman laughed. He came closer to Margaret and then sat down on the grass beside her. He removed his hat and smoothed his long hair, a little sweaty from his walk. The gentleman then leaned forward and began assisting Margaret with her task, pulling up the dead vines and placing them in her basket.

"Oh, Rupert! Is that you?" yelled Mrs. Dashwood from the kitchen window. "It's been so long, my dear boy! I see that the springtime has finally brought you back 'round to us."

Mrs. Dashwood then retreated back into the kitchen, probably now preoccupying herself with setting an elaborate tea for their visitor.

"I am sorry I have not written for a while," said Rupert, now looking at the ground.

"Oh, it's nothing," said Margaret. "I expected that it would be quite a while before I heard from you. After all, you've had quite a year."

"An understatement," he replied. "The dissolution of the marriage was finalized a few months ago. Apparently, Mr. Walter Brooke had the resources to speed the petition through the courts. He did such a fine job with it that it is almost as if I were never married at all."

"And yet you were," she said.

"I was," said Rupert, "but all of that is over now. Cecelia has installed herself as Mr. Brooke's new wife in France. In all honesty, I do hope that she is happy. I wish her no ill will."

"Of course not," said Margaret. "It was harsh what she did, but people do move on."

"Indeed," smiled Rupert. "I made no progress on the book at all. My dean will perhaps be understanding, but we'll have to see."

"You still have the rest of spring and summer," offered Margaret. "I'm sure you could come up with something in the interim. You are a motivated soul, Rupert Smith; I feel positive that you will not return to the university empty-handed."

"You have always believed in me," said Rupert. "I wonder what I have done to deserve your friendship."

"Oh, I can tell you the answer to that exactly," said Margaret, smiling. "Never once have

THE OTHER DASHWOOD SISTER

you asked me to be anything other than what I am — loud, opinionated, independent, and proud. You have never tried to constrain me. You have only let me exist on my own terms. Speaking as a woman, I must impress upon you what that means, Rupert."

"I see," he said. "Then you will be quite pleased with the gift I have brought you." He smirked a little while searching in his satchel. After a moment, he pulled out a small parcel, wrapped in brown paper and tied up with twine.

"Instead of working on my book," he explained, "I've been wound up in the work of this little project. I realized its necessity back before Christmastime, and I've put all my energy into bringing it to fruition. It was not necessarily a distraction — it was exactly the right way to spend my time."

Margaret looked at the little parcel quizzically. She always welcomed presents, but this tiny package seemed like it was not much to show for so many months of work, as Rupert claimed.

"Rupert, what is it?" asked Margaret.

"Open it and see," he said, as he pushed the small package closer to her.

When she pulled the twine loose and unfolded the paper, the object inside confused her. She did not know what to make of it. It was a small book, beautifully bound in an emerald green cloth cover. Though it was small, the pages themselves seemed hefty, and only when she lifted it out of its wrapping did she notice the gold lettering on the front of the book.

What she read stopped her breath entirely.

The gold lettering communicated the subject of the book quite clearly:

**CONSIDER THE WOMEN:
AN ACADEMIC EXAMINATION OF
SHAKESPEARE'S FEMALE CHARACTERS**

BY

M. DASHWOOD

Margaret, above all things in the world, loved to be *surprised*, but she was rarely so surprised that her lungs were rendered breathless. Margaret did not know what to say. All she could do was stare at the little green book before her and try to remember how to breathe. As if the cover of the book was not proof enough of what she held in her hands, she quickly cracked it open to consider its contents. Inside, she found the essays she had written to Rupert while he traveled in search of his estranged wife. She had never expected to see these essays again; her only real intention in writing them was to distract her friend with talk of books, something he desperately needed while his life was falling apart.

As she read over the chapter headings, she felt the shock of seeing her words in print. It was only then that she realized how much work must have gone into editing, arranging, and producing such a book as this.

She locked eyes with Rupert. "My dear friend, what have you done? Have you published this book yourself?"

He smiled. "I only served as agent. The essays you sent were extraordinary. I knew that they were only meant for me, but I felt they must be shared. A colleague of mine is connected to a small scholarly press that was acquiring new titles, and I asked if the collection of essays I possessed would be sufficient for a small book. After reading them, he heartily agreed. Your book, Margaret, has come into existence by your will alone. I only served as midwife."

After a pause, he added, "I wish we could have published it with your full first name, but I'm afraid the world is not quite ready for a female Shakespeare scholar. For now, you will have to remain M. Dashwood among academic circles."

"Truthfully, Rupert," she said, "I would rather be judged by the content of my ideas — let the revelation of my womanhood be saved for in-person encounters with the guild of scholars." She smiled at the thought of *surprising* a roomful of academics with her obvious femaleness. The possibility of such a spectacle was almost as grand a gift as the book itself.

"This is why you have not written lately, isn't it?" she asked.

"I'm afraid so," he said. "It took quite a long

time to transcribe and edit your abominable handwriting, and then, of course, the pages must be proofed before the final printing. It is a good book, Margaret. I am afraid it won't make you rich — scholarship never does — but the work does you great credit."

"Thank you, Rupert," said Margaret, with all the earnestness she could muster. "This is far more than I ever could have imagined."

"I have only tried to do what is right," he said.

Margaret decided that the time had come. She removed her bonnet and, with the tiny book sitting on her lap, addressed Rupert with all her assertiveness and power.

"Rupert," she began, "I have given a great deal of thought to my future lately. And I feel that, in order for it to be as glorious and vibrant as possible, my future must find itself linked to yours."

"Margaret, what do you mean?" asked Rupert.

"Rupert, before you came to the village for your sabbatical, I resolved to spend the year contemplating whether we ought to get married. I concocted an entire method for deciphering if the match was a good one, and I poured a great deal of thought into planning how I would take stock of the depth of my feelings. Of course, my plans were rather thwarted when you arrived with a wife in tow. But the past year of my life has taught me a great deal about what love looks like *for me*.

I was so frustrated that I had never experienced the overwhelming sensation of being in love, and I was determined to access it — especially when I felt jealousy over you getting to it first."

"Margaret…," interrupted Rupert.

"No, please let me finish." She narrowed her gaze until it seemed to pierce him with understanding. "What I learned is that love feels quite different for me than it appears in novels. Indeed, my experience of love is outlandishly different from what my older sisters have lived. I may feel stirrings of extreme warmth toward another person, but what love *truly* looks like for me is a state of faithful patience. I never thought that I would wait for anyone. But when you brought Cecelia home as your wife, I understood intuitively that I would wait for you, no matter how long, even if the time never came where I would be yours." She took his hand and brushed his windblown hair out of his face. "I would do it all again, my darling. But, please, don't make me wait any longer. I would like to marry you, and I would prefer it to take place before the end of spring."

Rupert was dumbstruck. He stared at her silently, attempting to digest the fact that Margaret had just proposed to *him*. Margaret sat quietly while he seemed to compose his reply in his mind. But there came a point where she lost her patience.

"Rupert, *do* say something," she implored. "I understand that I must seem rather forward, but, honestly, would you expect anything less from me? And please don't tell me I am mistaken in believing that you love me just as much as I love you."

After a pause, he finally spoke. "You are not mistaken."

He leaned in close to her face, and, skipping her lips, placed a soft kiss on the scar on her forehead.

And then Margaret Dashwood flung her arms around her dearest friend and greatest love, overjoyed to finally have the sensation of recognition that comes from two independent souls acknowledging that they are inextricably linked. And when Rupert kissed her, Margaret felt all the hardened muscles of her neck and back relax into a state of comfort she had not previously believed existed. In the warmth of the sun, the two friends held one another with the strength of two people who did not wish for a moment to end.

When they finally pulled apart from each other, Rupert asked, "But what of John Willoughby? I was under the impression that the two of you were rather attached to one another. Indeed, I had heard a rumor that he intended to propose marriage — did he play the rogue with you, Margaret?"

Margaret laughed at the thought. "Play the rogue? Oh, no!"

"Then what happened, my darling?" said Rupert, as he gripped her hand.

"John Willoughby did tender me an honest proposal of marriage," explained Margaret. "And, although I found him charming and felt a great deal of warmth toward him, I concluded that those feelings were not necessarily sustainable. I was indeed prepared to love him in spite of his flaws and past sins, but I had considerable doubts as to whether he could love the sins within me."

"And so you rejected him?" asked Rupert.

"Gently — but, yes, I rejected him," said Margaret. "It is unfortunate, actually. I doubt he will ever speak to me again. He was rather frustrated with me when I gave him my final answer, but I had taken plenty of time to make sure that my answer was correct. I stand by it wholeheartedly."

"You are quite sure you are not in love with John Willoughby?" asked Rupert.

"Oh, quite."

"Then I will never speak of it again, dear Margaret." And then he scooped her up once more in his arms and buried his face in her neck, overcome with joy over the extraordinary person who had just proposed to him.

"Margaret," continued Rupert, "I take it this means you know I have loved you all along."

"I never acknowledged it explicitly," she replied, "but all of the evidence suggested that it was true. To be honest, Rupert, I have been so afraid of repeating the mistakes of my older sisters that I did not have space enough in my heart to truly consider marriage."

"I believed that you would never come around to me," he said. "And so I married Cecelia when she showed the slightest bit of interest. I do not regret that decision — I was ready to be married, and I acted honestly at the time — but I see now that I am equally to blame for mine and Cecelia's poor match."

"It matters not," said Margaret warmly. "All that matters is that we finally found the means to be honest with each other. That is what I hope for the most for our marriage, Rupert."

He kissed her scar again and then her lips.

"I will marry you before spring's end," he whispered into her ear.

"We will marry *each other*, my darling" corrected Margaret.

From the kitchen window, Mrs. Dashwood — who had been spying on them the whole time — thought the time had now come for her to speak.

"Would the two of you fancy some tea?" she yelled from the window. "I have a sense that you have much to tell me this afternoon, and I will not be denied a full explanation!"

"Coming, Mother!" called Margaret.

Before rising to go inside, Margaret surveyed the face of her future husband and felt a swell of comfort surge from inside her heart. The man whom she loved was one who respected her, and she felt confident that she was dutifully following her sisters' advice. Once more, Margaret took the small book — *her* book — in her hands and considered how it was a talisman of the honor that Rupert bestowed on her mind and her personhood. She wondered how many of her female peers experienced such a sensation of respect. She suspected that the number was much too low for her satisfaction. Gratefully, though, Margaret was not among their ranks. When she married, it would be to a man who saw the fullness of her humanity. She would, of course, accept nothing less.

The first to stand, Margaret reached down her hand to help Rupert to his feet.

***

In the end, marrying Rupert Smith had been an easy decision for Margaret Dashwood. And this ease portended that the match was destined for success. All were joyous over the two young people, even those who had not thought either Margaret or Rupert to be all that young to begin with. Mrs. Dashwood, in particular, was pleased that her third daughter had finally found love. It did not even bother her that Rupert Smith's fortune was rather modest. All that mattered was that Margaret was now settled, and Mrs. Dashwood looked forward to a future that included spending a great deal more time with her grandchildren.

Marianne and Elinor — as well as their husbands — were likewise satisfied with Margaret's choice. Both sisters had prepared themselves for Margaret to marry John Willoughby, but they were grateful that she had made a different choice. Neither of them believed that it was their words that had played a role in changing Margaret's mind; instead, they both understood that Margaret made decisions by herself. She did not need their help, only their support. Both Marianne and Elinor were proud of their sister, and copies of Margaret's books were lovingly placed in the libraries of both of their homes.

In general, the sisters were glad to never more think of John Willoughby, a man who seemed unable to fully leave the Dashwood women alone. Only Margaret felt a degree of pain for how she had disappointed him. She did not regret her words to him, but she nonetheless was sure she would never see the likes of him again. She suspected as much when, after declining his proposal, she watched him ride away into the wintery Christmas Eve.

After a honeymoon in Africa (at Margaret's insistence), Margaret and Rupert would live in London, within walking distance of the university. But Margaret insisted that they make some sort of plans for remaining in the country when the summer months arrived. They need not always live in the city, especially when the university was not in session. She kindly reminded Rupert, too, that she had been promised the opportunity to work alongside him — and she suspected that they both would be much more efficient in the country air. Margaret's greatest wish was that, of all the houses they might lease in the country, there could be no other choice than the cottage in which she had grown up. And Rupert had no intention of denying his beloved.

Margaret Dashwood waited for no gentleman — except for *one*. And it seemed he had long waited for her, as well.

But on her wedding day, a different gentleman was waiting for quite another event. From a hilltop overlooking the church and its grounds, a tall man on an old mare stood like a sentinel. His face was indifferent to the pastoral scene before him, and he absentmindedly stroked the neck of his elderly horse. His eyes were fixed on the doors of the church.

When the old doors swung upon and out poured the happy bride and groom, he quickly turned his eyes toward the sun and rode away.

Made in United States
Troutdale, OR
12/26/2023